She found the suite without difficulty. There was a notice attached to the door handle, stating "Please do not disturb."

I bet, thought Kate, bitterness clenching her throat. She flung the door wide and marched in.

Ryan had risen to his feet and was looking at her, head thrown slightly back, his eyes hooded. He said quietly, "Hello, Kate."

She had planned it all on the walk here. She was going to be dignified—civilized. She was not going to break down, or make a scene. But at the sight of him—his self-possession when she was falling apart—something exploded in her head. Her voice when it emerged was on the edge of a scream.

"Don't you dare say 'Hello' to me. Don't you dare. I'm pregnant, do you hear me? Pregnant."

SARA CRAVEN was born in South Devon, England, and grew up surrounded by books, in a house by the sea. After leaving grammar school she worked as a local journalist, covering everything from flower shows to murders. She started writing for Mills & Boon in 1975. Apart from writing, her passions include films, music, cooking and eating in good restaurants. She now lives in Somerset.

Sara Craven has recently become the latest (and last ever) winner of the British quiz show *Mastermind*.

Books by Sara Craven

Don't miss any of our special offers. Write to us at the following address for information on our newest releases.

Harlequin Reader Service
U.S.: 3010 Walden Ave., P.O. Box 1325, Buffalo, NY 14269
Canadian: P.O. Box 609, Fort Erie, Ont. L2A 5X3

SARA CRAVEN

Marriage Under Suspicion

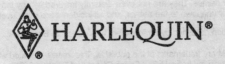

HARLEQUIN®

TORONTO • NEW YORK • LONDON
AMSTERDAM • PARIS • SYDNEY • HAMBURG
STOCKHOLM • ATHENS • TOKYO • MILAN • MADRID
PRAGUE • WARSAW • BUDAPEST • AUCKLAND

ISBN 0-373-12058-3

MARRIAGE UNDER SUSPICION

First North American Publication 1999.

This edition published by arrangement with Harlequin Books S.A.

® and TM are trademarks of the publisher. Trademarks indicated with
® are registered in the United States Patent and Trademark Office, the
Canadian Trade Marks Office and in other countries.

Visit us at www.romance.net

Printed in U.S.A.

CHAPTER ONE

THIS, Kate decided, as she crossed the deserted hotel lounge, had quite definitely been the morning from hell.

She sank into a chair by the window, easing off her elegant black court shoes under the shelter of the table, and discreetly massaging the ball of one aching foot against the calf of her other leg.

Outside on the sunlit lawn, the pretty pink and white striped marquee, with its distinctive octagonal shape, was being swiftly and efficiently dismantled.

Kate, recalling how many hours and telephone calls had been required to track it down, surveyed the operation with genuine regret.

Elsewhere in the hotel, all preparation on the carefully chosen menu for two hundred and fifty people had ceased; the champagne was being returned to the cellar, together with the claret and the chablis; and phones were buzzing as disappointed guests were told their presence would not be required after all.

Kate sighed soundlessly, and opened the file in front of her, running a finger down a hastily assembled check list. Setting up a wedding was a long and complicated business. Cancelling it on the day itself was almost as complex, and probably twice as hectic.

Damn Davina Brent, she thought irritably, scanning

through the invoices from her sub-contractors. Why couldn't she have decided a month—a week—even yesterday—that she didn't want to go through with it?

Quite apart from the drama and upset of the last few hours, she would also have saved her distraught family some massive but unavoidable bills.

It was the first time since Kate and Louie, her friend from college days, had started Special Occasions that a bride had actually cried off on her wedding morning. In fact, in the three years that they'd been functioning, they'd had remarkably few hiccups, organising other people's parties, receptions and special events.

And certainly there'd been no prior hint that the beautiful Davina was likely to throw such a spectacular last-minute wobbly. During the preliminary discussions that Kate had had with her, and her unfortunate husband-not-to-be, and, indeed, ever since, she'd seemed very much in love.

But then, thought Kate with an inward shrug, how could you tell what went on in other peoples' lives— or heads?

For a moment, she was very still, aware of an odd shiver tingling down her spine. A goose walking over my grave, she thought. Or an angel passing over.

And jumped, as a glass was placed on the table in front of her. A martini, if she was any judge, and served just as she liked it, very dry, very cold, and with a twist of lemon. Only, she hadn't ordered it.

'There must be some mistake,' she began, turning in her chair to face the waiter. Instead she found herself looking up into the unsmiling face of Peter Henderson, the erstwhile best man, now casually clad in jeans and sweater.

'No mistake at all.' His voice was terse. 'You look as if you need a drink. I know I do.' He indicated the whisky glass he was holding.

'Thanks for the thought.' Kate accorded him a brief, formal smile. 'But I make a rule—no alcohol while I'm working.'

He grimaced. 'I thought, under the circumstances, you'd be off duty by now.'

Kate gestured at the open file. 'There are still a few loose ends to tie up.'

'May I join you, or will I be getting in the way?'

'Of course not. Sit down—please.' Kate searched around under the table with a stockinged foot for her discarded shoes.

'Allow me.' Peter Henderson went down on one knee, and deftly replaced the errant footwear before seating himself in an adjoining chair.

'Thank you.' Kate was aware of a faint, vexed flush warming her face.

'No problem.' He surveyed her, his expression openly appreciative of the dark blonde hair, drawn sleekly back from her face, and the slender figure set off by her elegant raspberry-pink suit, and black silk shirt. He reached across the table, touching his glass to hers.

'What shall we drink to?' he asked lightly. 'Love and happiness?'

'Under the circumstances, that could be something

of a minefield,' Kate said drily. 'Let's stick to something brief and uncomplicated like "Cheers."' She paused. 'How is your brother?'

His mouth tightened. 'Not good. Shattered, in fact.'

'I can believe it.' Kate hesitated again. 'I—I'm so sorry.'

He gave a slight shrug. 'Maybe it's all for the best. If one has genuine misgivings, a clean break now could be preferable to a messy divorce later, when children could be involved, and real damage done.'

'I suppose so,' Kate agreed slowly. 'But they seemed so genuinely well-suited. Did he have any idea she was having second thoughts?'

'I imagine any problems would be simply attributed to bridal nerves.' He looked at the narrow gleam of platinum on her wedding finger. 'A pitfall you apparently managed to avoid.'

She said lightly, 'Goodness, it's so long ago, I can hardly remember.'

'Not that long, surely, unless you were a child bride.'

'Oh, please.' Kate sent him an ironic look, aware that she'd flushed again. 'It was actually five years.'

'A lifetime.' He sounded amused. 'Any regrets?'

'None at all,' Kate returned sedately. 'We're very happy. Extremely so,' she added, wondering why she'd needed the extra emphasis.

'Any children?'

She was aware, once again, of his blue eyes assessing her trim figure.

'Not yet. We're both busy establishing our careers.'

She picked up the waiting martini, and sipped it after all, relishing its forceful chill against her dry throat. 'In Ryan's case a change of career,' she added.

'Something you don't approve of?'

'On the contrary.' Kate stiffened. 'What makes you think that?'

'The fact that you took a drink before you mentioned it.'

She laughed. 'You made a wrong connection, I'm afraid. The actual fact is that martinis are my weakness in life.'

'The only one?'

'I try to limit them,' she said drily.

'Would calling me Peter be regarded as a weakness?'

She was suddenly conscious of a marginal shift in her body language—that she'd relaxed—turned towards him. She straightened, giving him a cool look. 'An error of judgement, possibly.'

She picked up her file, shuffling some papers. 'And not very businesslike,' she added crisply.

'But your business isn't with me. Like you, I'm just trying to pick up the pieces.'

'In that case, shouldn't you be with your brother instead of me?'

'Andrew's with our parents. They're taking him home with them for a few days.' He frowned at his glass. 'I don't know if that's a good thing, or a bad. My mother's inclined to be rather emotional, and she's never been a fan of Davina's anyway. It might make any rapprochement a bit difficult.'

Kate's brows lifted. 'You really think that could happen—in spite of everything?'

'Perhaps—if they're left to come round without too much interference on either side.' He sighed. 'In fact I wouldn't be surprised if they just sloped off to a registry office one day, and simply got married in front of a pair of witnesses off the street. Neither of them wanted this kind of shindig in the first place. I wonder if it was the pressure of it all that finally goaded Davina into flight?'

'I do hope not.' Kate swallowed the rest of her martini and put down the glass. 'Or I might develop a guilt complex.'

'Blame both sets of parents,' he said succinctly. 'They were the ones coming up with endless lists of people who simply had to be invited.'

'They usually are,' Kate agreed. 'And I must admit I'd have hated it myself.'

'You mean you didn't have the bridal gown, the fleet of cars, and the cast of thousands—when you're actually in the business?'

She smiled constrainedly. 'Ah, but I wasn't then. And we did exactly what you recommended for Andrew and Davina. A registry office early in the morning, with two witnesses.'

'Followed by unmitigated bliss?'

'I would never claim that.' Kate frowned. 'I wouldn't even want it. It sounds deadly dull.'

'So you and Mr Dunstan enjoy the occasional clash?'

She shrugged. 'Naturally. We're both individuals in

a relationship which pre-supposes a fair degree of to-getherness, and all kinds of adjustments.' She paused. 'And it isn't Mr Dunstan. That's my name. My husband's called Lassiter.'

His brows lifted. 'You mean you're married to Ryan Lassiter—the writer?'

Kate smiled. 'I do indeed. Are you one of his fans?'

'Actually, yes.' Peter Henderson seemed momentarily nonplussed. 'I started life as a City broker myself, so I read *Justified Risk* as soon as it came out. I thought it was amazing—that combination of big business and total chill. And the second book was just as good, which doesn't always happen.'

'I'll tell him,' Kate said lightly. 'Fortunately a great many people share your opinion.'

'Is he working on a third book?'

She shook her head. 'On a fourth. The third's already in the pipeline for publication this autumn.'

'I can't wait. And while he's pounding the keyboard you do this?' Peter Henderson reached across and picked up one of her business cards which had slipped out of the file. 'And all under your own name too,' he added softly.

Kate shrugged again. 'We might have fallen on our faces. It seemed a good idea to keep our individual enterprises totally separate.'

'But now you're flying high, surely?'

'Let's say we're holding our own in difficult trading times.' Kate closed her file. 'Please keep the card, in case you have a celebration of your own to plan one of these days.' She sent him a mischievous look. 'Maybe even a wedding reception.'

'God forbid.' He shuddered.

'You're against marriage?'

'Not for other people,' he returned. The blue eyes dwelt on her thoughtfully. 'Although I'd have to make exceptions there too.'

Their glances locked—challenged—and to Kate's shock she was the first to look away.

What's the matter with me? she thought, swallowing. I'm an adult woman. I've been chatted up before, plenty of times. Why should this be any different?

With what she recognised was a deliberate effort, she retrieved her black briefcase from the floor beside her, snapped open its locks, and put away the file with an air of finality.

As she got to her feet, she gave Peter Henderson a brief, noncommittal smile.

'Well, thanks for the drink. Now I must really get on.'

'Must you?' He pushed back his own chair, and rose. 'I was hoping, once you were free of your business cares, that we might have dinner together.' He paused. 'I've decided to stay on here tonight after all.'

'And I've decided to make the earliest possible start back to London.' Kate's tone was more curt than she'd intended.

'Running away, Miss Dunstan?' Peter Henderson's smile was engaging and unabashed. He glanced down at the card he was holding. 'Or may I call you Kate?'

'If you wish.' Her own glance was pointedly at her

watch. 'Although I can't see why you should wish to. Unless you do decide to throw a party one of these days, we're unlikely to meet again. Even if Andrew and Davina get together again, I doubt they'll hire our services a second time.'

Peter Henderson smiled at her. 'I remain an optimist,' he said. 'In all sorts of ways.'

He paused. 'And believe me—Mrs Lassiter—' he stressed the name almost mockingly '—if and when I decide to party, you will be the first to know.'

Kate felt suddenly as if her own parting smile had been painted on, as wide and foolish as a clown's.

She said quietly, 'Goodbye, Mr Henderson,' and walked away, out of the hotel lounge, without looking back.

She made her way straight to the powder room, glad to find it deserted. She closed the door behind her, and leaned on it for a moment, angrily aware that her breathing was flurried. Hoping too that her exit had been as dignified and final as she'd intended.

But I couldn't guarantee it, she thought, pulling a face. And he was probably well aware of it, damn him.

She walked to the row of basins, smoothed back her already immaculate hair, added another unnecessary coating of colour to her mouth, then washed her hands—a symbolic gesture which forced a reluctant laugh from her.

Admit it, Kate, she adjured her bright-eyed reflection, half guilty, half amused. Just for a moment there, you were actually tempted.

After all, Ryan isn't expecting you back until tomorrow. And it was only an invitation to dinner. Who would know if you'd accepted—and where would have been the harm anyway? Your marriage is rock-solid—isn't it?

For a moment, she was very still, conjuring up Ryan's image in her mind, until he seemed to be standing beside her, tall, loose-limbed, nose and chin assertively marked in a thin face that would always be attractive rather than handsome.

So real, she realised wonderingly, that she could almost smell the slightly harsh, totally male scent of the cologne he used. So sexy, in a cool, understated way, that her whole body clenched in sudden, unexpected excitement.

His long legs and narrow hips were encased in faded denim, his collarless shirt was unbuttoned at the neck, and the sleeves rolled back over muscular forearms. Working gear—and a far cry from the dark City suits he'd worn when they first met. But the changes in Ryan went far deeper than mere surface appearance. And if she was honest, this had been one of the aspects of his new life which had troubled her most.

As usual, one strand of his silky mid-brown hair was straying untidily across his forehead. But, less usually, the hazel eyes were narrowed almost questioningly, and the mobile mouth wasn't slanted with its usual amusement.

She was being watched, she thought slowly, by a cool, sexy stranger. With the accent on the cool.

Or she was simply transferring her guilt. She rallied herself with a slight shrug, acknowledging Ryan's reaction if he ever discovered she'd been tempted, even for a second, to accept Peter Henderson's invitation.

She closed her eyes, dismissing the image, wiping the whole incident. It had been a brief glitch on the smooth tenor of her life, not to be considered again.

Aloud, she said, 'It's time I went home.'

She used the public telephone in the foyer to call their flat. The answering machine was on, indicating that Ryan was working.

She said lightly, 'Hi, darling. The wedding's off, and I'll be back as soon as I can make it. Why don't we eat out tonight—my treat? See if you can get a table at Chez Berthe.'

She called at Reception on her way out to tell them she was leaving, and check that the cancellation hadn't brought any unexpected hitches.

'Everything's fine,' the girl assured her. 'It's just such a shame. None of us can remember it ever happening before.'

'I hope it doesn't set a trend,' Kate said drily as she turned away.

'Oh, one minute, Miss Dunstan.' The receptionist halted her. 'I almost forgot.' Her expression was suddenly conspiratorial—almost sly. 'This was left for you.'

She handed over an envelope, inscribed 'Ms Kate Dunstan' in bold handwriting.

'Thanks,' Kate said coolly, and thrust it into her bag, silently cursing the other woman's overt curiosity. It was important to leave the place on a business footing, she thought, pinning on a smile that was pleasant but formal.

'I can't foresee any further problems,' she said briskly, 'but if something does crop up you can contact me at the office or on my mobile.'

She waited until she was in her car before she opened the envelope. It was Peter Henderson's business card, but he'd scrawled his private number across the back of it.

And underneath he'd written, 'I told you I was an optimist.'

Kate's mouth tightened. She was sorely tempted to tear the card up and dump it in a waste bin, except there wasn't one handy. She'd get rid of it later, she decided, slotting the card into the back of her wallet. After she'd added him to the client file list in the office computer, of course, she amended. That would neutralise him. Reduce him to a business contact. Innocent, and potentially useful. End of story.

Traffic was miraculously light, and she didn't hang about, finding herself at home almost before she'd dared hope, parking next to Ryan's Mercedes in the underground car park which served the development where their flat was sited.

It was the top floor of what had once been a large warehouse, overlooking the river. In addition to a superb living area, which also contained the galley kitchen, a bathroom, and the room which Ryan used as his office, there was a wide gallery up a flight of wooden steps housing their bedroom, and a private bathroom. The floors were pale, sanded wood, the ceilings were high and vaulted, and every window had wonderful views.

Each time she opened the front door, Kate felt a thrill of ownership buzz through her veins. It was light years away from the flat they'd had when they first married, she thought. That had been the basement of a Victorian house, where the floors creaked, the windows stuck, and the plumbing was eccentric. They'd spent the first year furnishing it, prowling round second-hand shops and markets to find exactly the pieces they wanted. But the eclectic mixture they'd assembled wouldn't have fitted in here, and they'd sold most of it on to the couple who'd bought the basement from them as well.

Here, furnishings had been kept to a minimum, and clutter banished altogether. Kate had concentrated on shades of cream and ivory, with an occasional bold splash of Mediterranean colour. And it worked. A glossy magazine had suggested using the flat in a series on 'Working at Home', but rather to Kate's disappointment Ryan had refused to take part, saying simply he couldn't afford the disruption to his routine.

Now, she used her key quietly, because Ryan would still be working, and it was important not to disturb him. He liked peace when he was writing, although he was reasonably tolerant of interruptions, especially when they came with a cup of coffee.

I'll give him half an hour, and then take him some, Kate thought, dropping her briefcase on to a sofa.

And she paused, as it occurred to her that things were altogether too quiet, too peaceful. She listened intently, but only silence came surging back to her.

She cleared her throat. 'Ryan—are you there?' And, for the first time, was aware of a faint echo in all that vaulted emptiness.

She thought, in bewilderment, but he must be here. He's always here. And besides, he didn't take the car.

Across the room, she could see the answering machine's red light winking at her. When she played back the tape, she found just her own message, unheard.

She checked the bedroom, and both bathrooms, then looked in Ryan's office to see if he'd left her a note, but there was nothing. His desk was clear.

Of course, she thought. He wasn't expecting me until tomorrow.

She felt absurdly deflated. She'd rushed back here like a mad thing to be with him, and he was somewhere else. What was more, there was no table booked at Chez Berthe, or anywhere for that matter.

She sighed. She'd have to do something with pasta. Tuna, she thought, and anchovies, and there was some garlic bread in the freezer. She might as well make a start on it, because Ryan wouldn't be long—not if he hadn't taken the Merc.

On the other hand, she realised, as she glanced restively around her, the flat was preternaturally tidy—unused even, as if no one had been there all day.

Oh, stop it, she adjured herself. You're just disappointed. You don't have to be paranoid as well.

She went into the kitchen and filled the kettle. She'd make herself a cup of coffee instead, and then begin the evening meal. Surprise him when he returned.

As she turned off the tap, she saw the two crystal flutes upturned in the drainer.

Her brows lifted. Champagne? she thought. But Ryan hardly ever drank champagne. He was a claret man. They'd spent their eventual honeymoon touring the Médoc.

She set the kettle to boil, then obeying an impulse she hardly understood, flicked open the waste bin. An empty bottle of Krug was right there, mute evidence that Ryan had indeed been drinking champagne, and not on his own either.

For a moment, Kate stood staring down at it, then she dropped the lid and turned away.

Well, what of it? she thought, with a mental shrug. Clearly he had something to celebrate. Perhaps Quentin, his agent, had called round with news of the film option on the last book.

She still could hardly believe how spectacular Ryan's new career had proved. She'd thought he was firmly implanted in the City. Had been frankly horrified when he'd announced his decision to leave broking, and write his first novel. Kate, whose partnership with Louie had been in its early, tentative stages, had tried to reason with him, pointing out the risks he was taking, but he'd been quite determined.

'I don't like my life,' he'd said. 'I look at the people around me, and I can see myself becoming like them. I don't want that. This is my chance to break free, and I'm taking it.'

He'd added more gently, 'You don't have to worry, Kate. I've got money put away to cushion us initially. I won't let you starve.'

'I wasn't thinking of myself,' she'd protested. 'If you jack your job in, there's no way back. And becoming a writer is such a—leap in the dark. How do you know you can do it?'

'I'll never know, unless I try.'

'I suppose not.' She'd sighed. 'Well, do it, if you must. After all, we've always got Special Occasions to fall back on.'

There was a silence, then he'd said quietly, 'So we have. I was almost forgetting.'

But, in the event, it hadn't been needed. Ryan's script had been read and auctioned by Quentin Roscoe for a sum which had made Kate blink.

'You're a genius.' She'd flung her arms round Ryan, kissing him rapturously. 'Nothing can stop us now.'

Although it hadn't all been plain sailing, she was bound to admit. She still remembered the day Ryan had told her about the author tour which had been arranged in the States for the launch of *Justified Risk*.

'Every major city,' he told her jubilantly. 'Book signings, TV and radio interviews. And, while I'm working, you're going to be taken shopping and sightseeing.'

'I am?' Kate's smile faded. She bit her lip. 'Darling, I can't go with you.'

'What are you talking about? Of course you're coming. It's all arranged.'

'Then it'll have to be un-arranged,' Kate returned crisply. 'After all, I wasn't even consulted about this.'

'I wasn't included in the planning stage either,' Ryan said with a touch of grimness. 'These are the kind of hoops I'm expected to jump through, and be grateful. It's certainly the kind of opportunity you don't refuse.'

'Of course not, and I'm sure you'll be wonderful.' Even to her own ears, her voice held a slightly brittle note. 'But I'm far too busy at work to take that amount of time off.'

'Louie would understand—if you explained.'

'There's nothing to explain.' Kate lifted her chin. 'Like you, I have a career, Ryan—and a life. I'm not just an—appendage to be trailed round in your wake.'

'No indeed,' he said, too courteously. 'You're my wife, and I'm looking for a little support here.'

'So, I just drop everything and run?' Kate shook her head. 'I'm sorry, Ryan, but that isn't how it works.' She hesitated. 'Perhaps if I'd had more notice…'

'I've only just heard myself.' He paused 'Kate, I need you with me—please.'

'It's impossible,' she said stubbornly. She saw the utter bleakness in his face as he turned from her, and added hastily, 'Next time, maybe…'

'Of course,' he said expressionlessly. 'There's always a next time.'

Only there hadn't been. Ryan had carried out a number of promotional tours since, but she'd been included in none of them, although she could have accompanied him with Louie's goodwill.

'You're a fool,' her partner had commented when Kate had told her what had happened. 'If Ryan belonged to me, I wouldn't let him roam off alone.'

'He's not alone,' Kate had protested. 'He has people with him—a publicist, for one.'

'Male or female?' Louie had sent her a beady look. 'I don't know.'

'Then I'd get to know. I'm only a single woman, but it seems to me like the kind of information a caring wife should have at her fingertips.' Louie had adjusted her scarlet-rimmed spectacles. She was taller than Kate, and built on more Junoesque lines, with a mop of dark curly hair.

'Oh, don't be ridiculous,' Kate had said impatiently. 'I trust Ryan implicitly.'

Nevertheless, when Ryan got back she'd heard herself asking, 'How did you get on with the publicist?'

'Grant?' Ryan had shaken his head. 'Nice lad, but I think I was his first author. We carried each other.'

'Oh,' Kate had said, despising herself for feeling relieved.

The kettle whistled imperiously, bringing Kate back to the present with a start.

Not exactly the kind of trip down Memory Lane

that I wanted, she reflected wryly as she made her coffee.

And it must have been sparked off by her encounter with Peter Henderson. His questions had re-opened several cans of worms which she'd thought closed for ever, and that was vaguely disturbing.

So, she hadn't wanted Ryan to jettison his City career. She could hardly be blamed for that. But no one was more delighted than herself when the gamble paid off.

We're both doing what we want. We have a wonderful life, and a strong marriage, she told herself as she made her way back to the living area. Things really couldn't be better.

There was a small stack of mail beside the telephone, junk and bills by the look of it, she thought, wrinkling her nose as she flicked through the envelopes. There was only one she couldn't categorise quite so simply. An expensive cream laid envelope, typewritten, and addressed quite starkly to 'Kate Lassiter', with a central London postmark.

Kate slit open the envelope and extracted the single sheet of paper it contained.

She unfolded the letter, reaching casually for her coffee cup as she did so.

There was no address, and no greeting. Just two lines in heavy black script. Seven words which leapt off the page at her with a force that left her stunned.

Your husband loves another woman.

A Friend.

CHAPTER TWO

KATE felt totally numb. There was an odd roaring in her ears, while from a distance she heard the tinkle of crockery, and flinched from the scalding splash of liquid on her feet and legs.

She thought detachedly, I've dropped my coffee. I ought to get a cloth and clear it up before it stains the floor. I ought...

But she couldn't move. All she could do was read those seven words over and over again, until they danced in front of her eyes, reassembling themselves in strange meaningless patterns.

She felt her fingers curl round the paper, crushing it, reducing it to a tight ball which she threw, violently, as far as her strength allowed.

For a moment she stood, almost absently wiping her hands down the sides of her coffee-stained skirt, then, with a little choking cry, she bolted up to the bathroom where she was briefly and unpleasantly sick.

When the world had stopped revolving, she stripped off her clothes and showered, using water almost hotter than she could bear, as if scouring herself of some physical contamination.

Then she towelled herself dry, and re-dressed in leggings and a tunic.

She seemed to be looking at a ghost, she thought, as she combed her damp hair into shape. A white-faced spectre with shocked, enormous eyes.

Downstairs, she fetched a dustpan and cleaning materials, and set about cleaning up the spilled coffee, almost relishing the physical effort required to scrub at the stained floorboards. The cream rug was marked too, she noticed, frowning, and that would have to go to a specialist cleaning firm.

She stopped right there, with a tiny gasp. Her marriage was in ruins, and she was worrying about a bloody rug?

She knelt staring into space, aware of a deep inner trembling. Knowing that it was composed equally of anger and fear.

Heard her voice, hoarse and shaken, say, 'It's not true. It can't be true, or I'd have known. I'd have sensed something, surely. It's just a piece of random filth. Someone who hates us. Who's jealous of our happiness.'

The conclusion made her flesh crawl, but it was infinitely preferable to any other possibility, she realised, grimacing painfully.

She got to her feet, and took the china fragments into the kitchen for disposal. The champagne bottle in the wastebin jarred her. Before she could stop herself, she was standing by the sink, lifting the flutes to the sunlight, studying them minutely for any tell-tale signs of lipstick.

Oh, for heaven's sake, she derided herself. Don't let someone's malice turn you paranoid.

She put the glasses away, emptied the wastebin, and cleaned it meticulously. Then she deliberately made herself another cup of coffee, and carried it through to the living area, seating herself on one of the cream and maize striped sofas.

Normally, the panorama of the river fascinated her, the boats, the buildings which crowded the banks, the play of light on the water. Now, she gazed at it unseeingly, her mind running in aching circles, as she drank her coffee. It burned all the way down, but the inner chill remained.

She thought, I don't want this to have happened. I want everything back the way it was before...

In some ways, she wished she hadn't come home. That she'd accepted Peter Henderson's offer and stayed for dinner in Gloucestershire.

But that would have made no difference. The letter would still have been there, awaiting her eventual return.

She needed to find some way to deal with the situation. Work out some plan of action. Yet she felt totally at a loss.

She could always go for straight confrontation, she acknowledged, frowning. Just hand Ryan the letter and watch his reaction.

She put down the empty cup, and retrieved the

crumpled ball of paper from its corner, endeavouring to smooth out the creases.

I can't pretend to treat it lightly—make a joke of it, she thought. As soon as he sees what I did to it, he'll know it mattered—that it upset me. I can't let him know that. Not until I'm sure. One way or the other.

She stopped abruptly, with a small gasp, aware of how far and how fast she had come from her original total disbelief.

She found herself remembering an article she'd read in a magazine at the hairdressers. Titled 'His Cheating Heart', it had detailed some of the ways to check if a man was being unfaithful. And one of the chief danger signs, she recalled, her heart lurching sickly, had been long, unexplained absences.

She said aloud, huskily, almost desperately, 'Ryan—where the hell are you?'

No, she thought, setting her jaw. She would not let herself think like this. Five years of love and trust could not be destroyed by a single act of malice. She wouldn't allow it.

So she wouldn't mention the letter at all, she told herself, drawing a deep breath. In fact, she would make believe she had never seen it. That it didn't exist. She would make no wild accusations. Drop no veiled hints. She would act completely naturally, she thought fiercely. But—she would also be on her guard.

She tore the letter in half, then into quarters, before

reducing it to strips, and thence into a mound of minute fragments which she piled onto a saucer and burned.

She flushed the ashes down the sink, and wished the words could be erased from her mind with equal ease.

She chose a bottle of Ryan's favourite Bordeaux from the rack, and opened it. A nice, wifely gesture to welcome him home, she thought, biting her lip. Except there was no positive guarantee that he would be home...

If he didn't return, of course, that would be a whole new ball game. But she would deal with that only when she had to.

She sat curled up on the sofa, sipping her wine, and watching television, aware of the light fading from the sky above the river. But the words and images on the screen passed her by, as if she were blind and deaf. Her mind was occupied only by her own heavy thoughts.

It was with a sense of shock that she discovered that it was now completely dark, and realised how long she must have been sitting there. She uncoiled herself stiffly, forcing herself to move around the big room, switching on lamps, and drawing the voluminous drapes across the windows. Closing out the night, and the thousands of lights which twinkled at her like small prying eyes. Reinforcing the fact that she was still, unaccountably, alone.

She thought, with anguish, He's not coming back. And how am I going to bear it...?

The sudden sharp rattle of a key in the door made her wheel round, her heart pounding.

She said with a gasp 'R̶y̶a̶n? Oh, Ryan, it's you.'

'You were expecting someone else?' He spoke lightly, but the glance he directed at her across the intervening space was searching. He shut the door behind him, and put down his briefcase.

'Of course not, but I was getting worried. I didn't know where you were.'

'I'm sorry, but I didn't know you'd be around to worry.' His brows lifted questioningly. 'To what do I owe this unexpected pleasure?'

He was wearing, she noticed, his favourite pale grey trousers, topped by a white shirt, a silk tie in sombre jewel colours, and his black cashmere jacket. Not his usual casual weekend gear at all.

She swallowed. 'Oh, the bride got cold feet and cancelled. A Special Occasions first. All that lovely food, and the prettiest marquee in England, and no takers.' She realised she was beginning to babble, and bit her lip.

'Ah, well,' Ryan said lightly. 'It's probably a blessing in disguise. One less mistake to chalk up to experience. One less digit to add to the divorce statistics.'

She stared at him, suddenly and totally arrested. 'That's a very cynical viewpoint.'

'I thought I was just being realistic.' He paused. 'Did it cause you a lot of problems?'

'Enough.' Kate shrugged. 'But it also gave me the weekend back.' She hesitated in her turn. 'I did phone and leave a message. You must have been out all day.'

'Pretty well,' he nodded, discarding his jacket and tie and tossing them on to one of the sofas.

Kate watched him release the top buttons of his shirt with a swift, primitive yearning. How long was it since they'd last made love? It must be all of three weeks, she realised with an inward grimace. Just before she'd been taken ill with that twenty-four-hour tummy bug, when she thought back.

But I've been out a lot on business, she reminded herself defensively, and Ryan often works late into the evening, so that I'm asleep when he comes to bed.

But not tonight, she promised herself. Tonight, she would take infinite care to stay awake.

She smiled at him. 'Would you like a glass of wine? I—I didn't know what to do about food...?' She turned it into a question.

Ryan shook his head. 'I've eaten, thanks. But some wine would be good.'

She poured carefully, and handed him a glass. 'You look very smart.' She kept her tone casual. 'Have you been with Quentin?'

He shook his head. 'No, I had some research to do.'

'Oh.' Kate refilled her own glass and sat down. 'I thought you did that on the Internet.'

'Not all of it.' He didn't come to sit beside her, but prowled restlessly round the room. He paused by the phone. 'Have there been any other messages?'

'Apparently not.' Kate sipped her wine. 'Were you expecting anything in particular?'

'Not really,' he returned. 'There was some mail for you, by the way. Did you find it?'

'Yes,' she said. 'Oh, yes, thank you.'

He continued his pacing, then halted abruptly, his brows flicking together in a frown. 'What happened to the floor? And the rug?'

'That was me being clumsy.' She managed to laugh. 'I had a fight with a cup of coffee and lost. Does it look too obvious and awful? I'll get the rug cleaned, and there's some special stuff for the wood-work.'

'No, leave it,' Ryan said, his mouth twisting. 'I rather like the fact that we've actually put our mark on the place at last. I'd begun to think we were going to pass through without one blemish.'

'Pass through?' Kate echoed. 'That's an odd thing to say.'

He shrugged. 'Just a figure of speech.'

'And it's not "the place",' she went on, with a touch of fierceness, feeling uneasy, wanting, obscurely, to challenge him. 'It's a home. Our home.'

He laughed. 'Is it, my darling? I thought it was some kind of statement.'

'Can't it be both? Is it wrong for our environment to express who we are—our aspirations and achievements?' She could hear her voice rising.

'That,' he said, 'might depend on the aspirations and achievements. Although no one, seeing all this, could possibly doubt what a success we both are.' He lifted his glass in a mocking toast, swallowing the rest of his wine. *'Quod erat demonstrandum.'*

My God, she thought. We're almost quarrelling, and that's the last thing I want.

She put down her glass and went to him, sliding her arms round his waist, inhaling luxuriously the familiar male scent of his skin.

'Well, I love our success.' She spoke with mock-defiance, smiling up at him. 'And our happiness even more. And, as a bonus, we get to spend tomorrow together.' She traced the open neck of his shirt with her forefingers. 'Sunday, sweet Sunday, all by ourselves.' She lowered her voice temptingly. 'We can get up as late as we want. Walk in the park, or stay in with the papers. Find somewhere new to have dinner. Just like we used to.'

He shook his head. 'Sorry, my love, not tomorrow. I'm going down to Whitmead to have lunch with the family.'

'Oh?' Kate stiffened instantly. 'May I know when this was arranged?'

His voice was equable. 'My mother telephoned during the week.'

'You didn't mention it before.'

He gave her a meditative look. 'I didn't think you'd be particularly interested.'

He didn't add 'After the last time'. He didn't have to, Kate thought, wincing. The implication was right there.

She made her tone placatory. 'Darling, I didn't mean the stupid things I said on the way home. I— lost my temper. We both did.' She shook her head. 'I wish your mother could just understand that if and when we start a family it will be our own personal decision, taken when we're good and ready. And without any prompting.'

'It was just a casual remark, Kate. She didn't mean to interfere. Or start World War Three.' He paused. 'After all, when we first got married, a baby was very much on the cards. And we made no secret of it.'

'Yes, but everything changed when you gave up your city job,' Kate protested. 'I had to work while you established yourself as a writer. You know that.'

'I'm established now,' he said mildly.

'And so am I,' Kate reminded him. 'Which makes it more difficult now to find an appropriate time. Something that will fit in with our career demands. Surely your mother must see that.' She hesitated. 'And you remember what Jon and Carla Patterson were telling us about the nanny situation the other night. They've had one disaster after another.'

'So it seems.' His voice was noncommittal.

'Therefore it isn't something we can rush into,' she went on. 'And your mother has got your sister's children to fuss over, after all,' she added with a touch of defensiveness.

'Undoubtedly,' he agreed. 'But I can't promise she won't drop any more hints.' His mouth twisted slightly. 'I'm afraid we're just not a very reticent family.'

'Maybe not.' She pinned on a smile. 'So, does all this mean that I'm excluded from tomorrow's invitation?'

'On the contrary,' he said quietly. 'Everyone would be delighted to see you, but I assumed you'd be tied up at the office once you got back from Gloucestershire, and made your excuses.'

'You're quite right of course,' she agreed colourlessly. She detached herself from him, and turned away. 'I have got a load of paperwork to complete. So, next time, perhaps.'

'That might be best.'

Did she imagine it, or did he actually sound relieved?

My God, she thought, biting her lip. Am I really such a bitch?

She swung back towards him, smiling brightly. 'Shall we have some more wine?'

'I'd better not.' He sounded regretful. 'I need to keep a clear head.'

'You're not going to work tonight, surely?' Kate made no attempt to hide her disappointment.

'I have some editing to do. It won't take long.'

Kate knelt on the sofa, reaching forward to take his

hand. 'Couldn't it wait until the morning?' Her voice was husky, almost wistful. 'I—I've missed you.'

He shook his head. 'I've got to make an early start to Whitmead. I need to get it done now.' He disengaged his hand, then ran a finger down the curve of her cheek. 'I'll be as quick as I can.'

'Is that a promise?' Kate drawled the words, looking up at him through her lashes.

'Behave.' He bent and dropped a swift kiss on top of her head. 'I'll see you later.' He collected his briefcase and went into the office, closing the door behind him.

Kate stayed where she was for a moment, staring blankly in front of her, then she collected the wine glasses and took them into the kitchen to rinse them out. She could see her reflection in the window above the sink, pale-skinned, taut-mouthed, and wide-eyed.

She thought, with a sense of shock, I look—frightened.

And yet there had been nothing to be scared of—had there?

Admittedly, it hadn't been the ideal reunion under the circumstances. Ryan's reaction to her unexpected return hadn't been the one she'd hoped for. But then he was always preoccupied when the book he was working on reached a certain stage. Ordinarily, she wouldn't have given it another thought.

But life was no longer ordinary. The anonymous letter had changed all that. Those seven words had removed the certainties, and replaced them with doubts. And with the fear she saw in her own eyes.

He'd been doing research, he'd said. But what kind of research would he dress up for? And the meal he'd mentioned—had he eaten it alone?

Why didn't I ask him? Kate thought, twining a strand of hair round her finger in a gesture left over from childhood. Why didn't I find out exactly where he'd been? Got him to name the restaurant even?

Was it, maybe, because I didn't want to hear the answers? Because I was afraid to pursue them?

She shivered, and turned away from the strained face confronting her in the glass.

Ryan might not have been overwhelmed to see her, but they were hardly newly-weds, for heaven's sake. It didn't make him guilty of anything. And there was no real reason for him to change his plans either. They were both adults with their own lives.

And she could well do without a family Sunday at Whitmead, she told herself, pulling a face. The perfect roast, the home-grown vegetables, the seriously alcoholic trifle all ordained beforehand, and produced without a hitch, even when extra guests turned up, as they often did. The afternoon spent playing croquet or French cricket, or taking the dogs for a walk, to build up an appetite for the equally sumptuous tea. The noisy games of cards or Trivial Pursuit during the evening. It was all like a cliché of English country life.

Oh, come on, she chided herself. That really is

bitchy. You really don't want to go in case Sally and Ben are there with the children, and comparisons are drawn. Be honest about it. You don't want another row with Ryan on the drive back.

And she shouldn't be derogatory about Ryan's parents, even in thought, she added ruefully. Because she liked them both—even if Mrs Lassiter's warmth, charm and unbounded energy did make her feel slightly inadequate at times.

She simply wasn't used to the overt family affection, the candour about personal issues, the lively arguments, and the casual but whole-hearted hospitality.

Her own upbringing, she thought, had been so very different.

With a silent sigh, Kate wandered back into the living area, and stood for a moment, staring at the closed door to Ryan's office. There was nothing in the world to stop her crossing the space that divided them, of course.

She could open that door, go into that room, and ask how much longer he was going to be. She'd done it before, after all. And on more than one occasion she'd left her clothes on the floor first.

But even as her mouth curved in a reminiscent smile she knew she would not be doing so this evening.

When she'd gone to Ryan earlier, put her arm around him, he'd held her in return. But there'd been no passion in his response. No kindling intimacy in his touch. Once, he would have drawn her close against his body, found her mouth with his, his hands rediscovering all the sweet, sensuous routes to their mutual desire.

She had never before offered herself, and been rejected.

Although it hadn't been a real rejection, she assured herself quickly. After all, he'd said 'Later', hadn't he?

But, although this was later, she knew she wasn't going to risk it. She would let him set the parameters tonight.

She went up to the bedroom. In her lingerie drawer, she found the nightgown she'd bought the previous month on an impulse, but not yet worn. She unwrapped the layers of tissue and looked at it with satisfaction.

It was ivory satin, and classically simple, the bodice deeply slashed beneath shoestring straps, the skirt cut cleverly to cling.

Seductive, she thought, without being obvious. And there would never be a better time to try its effect.

She changed into it, brushed her hair loose over her shoulders, and added a breath of Patou's Joy to her throat, wrists and breasts.

Then, leaving one shaded lamp burning, she lay down on top of the bed to wait for him.

And we'll just see if he makes that early start for Whitmead, she thought, smiling to herself. Or if he'll have to ring his parents, and tell them he can't be there after all. Such a shame.

It was the kind of situation that usually she'd revel

in, but somehow she found it impossible to relax—to think herself into the appropriate frame of mind.

She was planning to ravish her own husband. She wanted him to find her warm and willing, not nerve-racked and clammy-skinned. She needed to feel anticipation, not uncertainty.

She found she kept turning her head restively towards the stairs, every sense alert for a sound, or sign of movement. But there was nothing. Ryan had said he wouldn't be long, but the time seemed endless.

She remembered the deep breathing learned at her Yoga classes at college, and its calming effect. She let herself sink into the mattress, counting silently to herself as she inhaled, held the drawn breath then slowly released it.

Gradually, she felt her inner tension ease, but at the same time her eyelids began to grow heavy.

Sleep, she thought drowsily. I mustn't go to sleep. I have to wait—wait for Ryan...

It was the cold that woke her eventually. She sat up with a shiver, one glance at the bed beside her telling her that she was still alone. The numbers on the clock radio informed her it was the early hours of the morning.

She slid off the bed, put on her robe and went downstairs.

Ryan was lying, fast asleep, on one of the sofas. Nearby the television still hummed gently, its screen blank.

Kate turned off the power, before bending over her husband, shaking his shoulder gently.

'Ryan,' she whispered. 'Darling, you can't stay here. Come to bed—please.'

He muttered something unintelligible under his breath, but he didn't stir, not even when she shook him again, harder.

She waited for a moment, then trailed slowly and defeatedly back to the gallery.

Even under the covers, the king-size bed felt frigid and unwelcoming.

She thought, So, he fell asleep in front of the television. It happens. It's no big deal.

And suddenly found that she wanted, very badly, to cry. Because it was a very big deal indeed.

CHAPTER THREE

KATE opened unwilling eyes to discover broad day-light. She sat up slowly, propping herself on an elbow, while she pushed her hair back from her face with her other hand, and looked around her, dazed from a rest-less night punctuated by brief, disturbing dreams.

The first thing she registered was that the pillow beside her was rumpled, and the quilt had been thrown back, indicating that Ryan had spent at least part of the night with her.

Well, she thought, that was something—even if he hadn't bothered to wake her.

She swung her feet to the floor, and padded across to the bathroom. Ryan's damp towel was hanging on the rail, and a pleasant aroma of cologne, toothpaste and soap pervaded the moist air. But he had gone.

As she turned away, disappointed, a faint but per-suasive scent of coffee invaded her consciousness, and she followed it down to the kitchen.

Ryan was standing at the worktop, buttering a slice of toast. He was wearing faded chinos with a plain white shirt. An elderly sweatshirt was draped round his shoulders, and his hair was still damp from the shower.

Kate leaned against the door jamb and watched

him, allowing, with a shrug of her shoulder, one of
the straps of her nightgown to slide down.

She said, softly, 'Hi, there.'

'Hi, yourself.' His smile was easy, widening as his
eyes surveyed her. 'You look positively delectable,
Mrs Lassiter. I don't think I've seen that particular
nightdress before.'

'You were meant to notice it last night.' Kate
smiled back at him, pleasurably aware that her nipples
were hardening under his scrutiny, and clearly out-
lined under the cling of the satin for his delectation.

'Sorry about that.' He didn't sound particularly re-
pentant. Nor did he come across to her as she expected. 'I worked longer than I intended, and then I
got interested in something on television. You know
how it is.'

She said, gently reproachful, 'You could have
woken me—when you came upstairs.'

'You were sleeping like a baby. I didn't have the
heart.' He took a pitcher of fresh orange juice from
the refrigerator, and poured her a glass. 'Your morning tonic, madam.'

'I can think of a far better pick-me-up than that.'
Kate spoke huskily, meeting his glance, knowing that
he liked seeing her like this, flushed and tousled from
sleep. She adjusted the strap of her nightgown, letting
her hands linger momentarily on her breasts. 'Why
don't we have—breakfast in bed?'

'I told you why last night.' He sounded faintly

amused. 'As soon as I've drunk my coffee, I'm off to Whitmead.'

'You've been invited to lunch.' She heard a pettish note in her voice, and tried to sound more beguiling. 'It surely won't take all morning for you to drive there.'

'Dad wants me to help him with some fencing.'

'Oh.' Kate straightened. 'And that naturally takes precedence over your wife?'

'It does today.' He set the glass of orange juice down on the worktop. 'You seem to have forgotten that you weren't even going to be here.'

He paused. 'Tell me, Kate, if the wedding had gone ahead, and I'd asked you particularly to come with me today, would that have taken precedence over the usual mopping-up operations?'

'That's not fair,' she protested. 'A wedding—or any kind of party—is entirely different. I set it up beforehand, and supervised the clearing-up afterwards. I don't have a choice in this. It's work.'

He shrugged. 'On the other hand, it could simply be a question of priorities. And today mine have been decided for me.'

He pushed the slice of toast to one side, untouched, and walked to the door. On the way past, he turned to her, his hands reaching for her wrists, pinioning her suddenly against the wall.

Kate gasped, half in indignation, half in excitement, as she twisted against his imprisoning grasp in an unavailing attempt to free herself.

Ryan's hazel eyes were unsmiling but intent as they looked into hers, watching her pupils dilate in anticipation, in the beginnings of an arousal she was powerless to control.

He leaned forward and kissed her slowly, almost insolently, his teeth grazing her lip, his tongue gliding against hers like heated silk.

Her response was immediate. Her mouth moved against his, sweetly, greedily. She lifted the hands which clasped hers, and placed them on her breasts.

She thought, exultantly, He's mine.

His leg parted her thighs, pressing the satin of her gown against the moist satin of her body in a deliberate, tantalising friction which forced a tormented moan from her throat.

She wanted him so fiercely that it hurt. She needed to feel him sheathed inside her—to be taken, there and then, against the wall, or on the floor. She wanted to see his cool, ironic control shattered in tiny pieces. To possess him, to know that he was as driven and desperate as she was herself.

Even when he stepped back, his breathing hurried and harsh, she thought she'd won.

She hooked her fingers under the straps of her gown, and pulled them down, letting the folds of satin slide down her body, and cascade around her bare feet. She waited, her nakedness a challenge, her body heated and ready for his invasion.

And saw him smile at her.

'Goodbye, darling,' he said softly. 'Don't ever think I wasn't tempted.'

He turned, and walked away from her towards the main door.

For a second, she was too shocked to move or speak. Then sheer outrage rescued her.

'Bastard,' she hurled after him, chokingly. 'Don't you dare walk out on me.'

But Ryan's only response was to blow her one mocking kiss as he left.

Kate closed down her computer, and switched off the power, sitting for a moment and staring at the blank screen. She could only hope that what she'd stored over the past hour made some kind of sense, but she guaranteed nothing.

For once, her mind had not been on the job in hand.

Instead, she'd found herself going over and over again the events of the past twenty-four hours, as if she were trapped on some weary treadmill.

And the inescapable and unpalatable fact facing her was that, leaving aside whether or not Ryan was actually having an affair, her own relationship with him seemed to have reached some kind of watershed.

Even now, she still could not quite believe the coolness of his rejection. Burned to think how he'd watched her offer herself, then walked away. How he'd left her standing there, naked, and ridiculous.

He'd spoken of temptation, but he'd found her attempted seduction all too easy to resist, she thought bitterly.

It was also clear he'd had not the slightest intention of taking her to Whitmead, even if she'd declared herself available.

Of course, I did say that hell would freeze over before I set foot in the place again, Kate remembered uneasily. But it was said in the heat of the moment. We were having a row for God's sake. He must know I didn't mean it.

Her mother-in-law's kindly probing about their intention to start a family must really have caught her on the raw, she thought, frowning. Because she'd had some unkind things to say about refusing to turn into a bloody baby farm like Sally, too.

Yet she liked her sister-in-law, and was fond of four-year-old Holly and eighteen-month-old Tom. But Sally, like her husband, had been a successful corporate accountant before she became a full-time mother, and Kate could only think, What a waste of a good brain, each time she saw her coping patiently with her lively toddlers.

Not that Sally had ever indicted by word or gesture that she wasn't totally happy with her new life. On the contrary.

And Ryan's right, Kate thought, grimacing. It was the life we had planned when we got married. The baby, the house in the country, the dogs—the whole bit.

Only our plan had to change, when Ryan risked

everything by changing his career. I simply had to work to give us some security, in case his gamble didn't pay off.

And now that my business is working well too I can't afford to pull out for family reasons. For one thing, it wouldn't be fair to Louie.

She paused. This was the moment when she usually added defensively, Besides—there's plenty of time ahead of us for all that.

Only it had suddenly occurred to her that perhaps this was no longer true.

Ryan, she thought. Ryan and another woman. Could it be true after all? Was this the reason behind his frankly dismissive attitude towards her?

After all, she only assumed he was in the flat working when she wasn't there. He could be anywhere—and with—anyone.

She felt as if someone had taken her by the throat, and was slowly tightening his grip.

The champagne glasses, she thought, leaning back in her chair. Why didn't I ask him about them? They'd have been the ideal excuse for a little probing.

The perfect time for a few teasing questions would have been after lovemaking, she told herself, with a sigh, when they were lying relaxed and fulfilled in each other's arms.

Only—it hadn't happened. And, if there was someone else, it might never happen again.

For the first time, she made herself face that unnerving possibility.

Never to touch him, she thought numbly. Never to feel his hands working their unique magic on her ecstatic skin. Never to welcome him into her body as the other half of herself in their own rapturous spiral to completion.

From the beginning of their relationship, Kate had found him a wonderful lover, intuitive, tender and exciting. Under his guidance, she'd explored the heights and depths of her own sexuality.

Even during the rocky moments that afflicted any new marriage, they'd always been united in bed, turning to each other passionately and without reserve, using their mutual desire to comfort and to heal.

But last night, and this morning, the talisman had failed to work. And she was frightened as well as humiliated.

Was that why Ryan had elected to go to Whitmead alone—to break the news to his family that he was ending his marriage? Could that be the reason some sixth sense had warned her that he didn't want her along?

And was she simply going to sit back and let it happen?

No, she thought. I'm bloody well not.

She took a frowning look at her watch. If she set off at once, she could be at Whitmead in time for lunch, and also, presumably, for any announcement that was going to be made.

So, they weren't expecting her, but the Lassiters' open-house policy would surely still apply to their daughter-in-law, she thought, her mouth twisting wryly.

It was a warm, sunlit day, and although traffic out of London was relatively heavy most of it was making for the coast. Kate headed inland for Surrey.

The Old Rectory was on the outskirts of the village, next to the parish church, a pleasant red-brick house, surrounded by a rambling garden, and a tall hedge.

The obvious thing to do was drive in through the gate, and park on the gravelled area which faced the front door, but for reasons she couldn't explain Kate decided to leave her car in a layby a short distance away, and arrive at the house on foot.

As she got nearer, she found her footsteps slowing, and she turned up the narrow lane which led to the side gate. As usual, all the doors and windows of the house were open, and Kate stepped on to the verge, keeping close to the hedge. She wanted, she realised uncomfortably, to see the lie of the land, before she, herself, was seen.

She paused suddenly, aware that something wasn't right.

She bent, parting the twigs of the beech hedge with urgent fingers, and peering through the curling leaves. Parked in front of the house, she saw Mrs Lassiter's Mini, and the elderly Jaguar that was her husband's pride and joy. Next to them was Ben and Sally's estate car, as expected. But there was no sign of Ryan's Mercedes anywhere.

My God, she thought, he's not here. He told me he was coming to Whitmead just to put me off. He's somewhere else—seeing someone else.

She straightened hurriedly, feeling sick, wincing as the beech twigs tangled in her hair, then froze as an excited yapping started up on the other side of the hedge, followed by a deeper, more persistent baying.

She'd forgotten about the all-hearing ears of Thistle the Cairn terrier, and Algernon the basset-hound. So much for secrecy, she thought bitterly. She'd better make a dash for it, back to her car before the dogs alerted someone in the house.

'Why are you hiding in the hedge, Aunty Kate?'

With a stifled groan, Kate glanced towards the side gate, almost scalping herself as she turned her head, to see Holly standing on the bottom bar peering over at her.

'I'm not hiding,' she returned mendaciously, painfully disentangling herself. 'I—I thought I heard a cat crying, and went to look.'

'Algy doesn't 'low cats,' Holly informed her austerely.

'Then I must have been mistaken.' Kate forced a smile, rubbing her head. 'It doesn't matter.'

'Are you coming to lunch?' Holly asked.

'I—think so.' Offhand, Kate could see no way of getting out of it, as Holly was sure to report her presence as soon as she got back to the house. But, in Ryan's absence, what possible excuse could she give for being there?'

'Does Grandma know?'

'Not yet.' Kate unlatched the gate, steadying Holly as she let it swing open. 'Let's go and tell her.'

With Holly scampering beside her, and the dogs at their heels, she went across the lawn and round to the back of the house.

As she'd expected, she found Mary Lassiter occupied in the kitchen, surrounded by a plethora of delicious smells, and enjoying the company of her younger grandchild, who was totally absorbed in a greyish piece of pastry that he was modelling into various shapes.

'Kate?' Mrs Lassiter's indulgent smile faded slightly as her daughter-in-law entered, to be replaced, fleetingly, by a look of apprehension. 'What—what a nice surprise,' she added weakly. 'I gathered from Ryan that work was keeping you in London.'

'I managed to get through it quite quickly.' Kate was conscious that this was the most muted welcome she'd ever received at Whitmead. 'So here I am,' she went on with spurious brightness. 'I—I hope it's not inconvenient.'

'No, oh, no,' Mrs Lassiter assured her without any particular conviction. She cast a harassed glance at the kitchen clock. 'Ryan's driven the others into the village to collect the papers, and buy some more wine.'

'Oh.' Kate felt almost weak-kneed with relief. 'I was wondering what had happened to him.'

'I expect they'll call in at the Crown, if you want

to go after them.' Mary Lassiter frowned. 'I didn't hear your car.'

'I parked down the road,' Kate admitted, hoping she wouldn't be called on for an explanation, and feeling more awkward with every moment that passed.

'I see,' Mrs Lassiter said vaguely. 'Well, would you keep an eye on Tom for me, dear, while I go and set another place? And make sure Algy doesn't steal any of the sausage rolls I've made for tea,' she added, giving a warning look at the basset, who stared mournfully back.

Kate sat down at the table, and looked at Tom's lump of pastry.

'That looks nice,' she said. 'Is it a cake?'

'No, silly, it's a monster,' Holly said scornfully. 'Tom likes monsters.'

'Like monsters,' agreed Tom, with his blinding smile, splattering the pastry on to the board.

Kate grinned back at him, wishing at the same time that she felt more at ease with the pair of them. But perhaps she didn't see enough of them, she thought. And, an only child herself, she had very little experience of young children, and their total unexpectedness.

She took a small piece of dough, and began to shape it into a rose, remembering how her mother used to do the same thing to decorate her pies.

'I need to go,' Holly announced suddenly, standing on one leg. 'And Grandma's shut the door, so I can't get out.'

'Oh.' Kate was taken aback. 'Well, I'll open it for you.' She paused. 'What about the cloakroom door?'

Holly wriggled. 'I don't know.'

'I'll come with you and make sure,' Kate told her reassuringly.

She wasn't allowed to accompany Holly into the cloakroom itself, being told very politely, to her relief, that her niece could manage all by herself.

She was waiting outside when she heard a faint ting from the hall phone, indicating that a receiver had just been replaced elsewhere in the house.

She looked up, and saw Mrs Lassiter coming down the stairs, looking preoccupied.

Kate thought, She's been making a phone call upstairs—where she wouldn't be overheard. To Ryan—to tell him I've arrived? But why should she? Unless, of course, Ryan didn't come down alone. And she instantly castigated herself for being not simply paranoid, but ridiculous.

The Lassiters were kind parents, but quite conventional in their outlook. While Ryan remained married to herself, they would never encourage him to bring some other woman to meet them.

She said quietly, 'Holly's in the cloakroom. I'd better get back to check up on Algy.'

'Oh, please, dear.' Mrs Lassiter shook her head. 'The last time I left him alone, he ate a dozen jam tarts, and a cheese and onion flan.' She shuddered. 'I don't know which was worse—the crime or the consequences.'

When Kate got back to the kitchen, Algy was sitting by the door, looking the picture of innocence. Only the crumbs still clinging to his heavy jowls gave him away.

'You're a terrible thief,' Kate told him severely, noting thankfully that he'd only got away with a couple of the sausage rolls.

'Thief,' echoed Tom, gleefully, as she sat down again beside him.

Algy thumped his tail in agreement, then wandered over, dumping his chin on her knee so he could drool on to her taupe linen trousers.

'Adding insult to injury.' She scratched the top of his head, and smoothed her hand down the long, velvety ears.

Tom was getting restive, bored with his pastry, so, after a while, she took him into the garden, the basset padding loftily behind them.

A wrought-iron table and chairs had been set under the shade of a tree. On the table was a tray containing a covered pitcher of home-made lemonade and some glasses, and under it was Thistle, panting gently. Nearby a rug had been spread on the lawn, with several toy cars and a plastic tub of Lego.

Kate guided Tom towards these distractions, then sat at the table and poured herself some lemonade, hoping its freshness would dispel the scared, dry feeling in her throat.

The sun was dappling down through the leaves, and the air was full of the scent of freshly cut grass. The murmur of traffic in the distance was almost drowned by the busy hum of bees at work in the herbaceous border.

Almost in spite of herself, Kate found she was drawing a deep, satisfied breath, and lifting her face to the warmth as the peace of the garden worked its magic on her, and some of her inner tension began to dissipate.

It wasn't how she'd normally choose to spend a Sunday, she thought drily, with two dogs snoring under her chair, and a very small boy playing motorways a few yards away, but it had its compensations.

When Tom brought the Lego tub over to her, she thought he simply wanted it to be opened for him, but he tugged at her hand, making it vigorously clear that he expected her to join him on the grass.

'No, Tom.' She detached herself gently. 'Go and play nicely.'

But 'nicely' wasn't a word in his vocabulary. The round, solemn little face darkened ominously and he let out a thwarted roar.

'He wants you to build him a garage,' said Holly, the faithful interpreter, appearing from nowhere.

'Does he now?' Kate said grimly. She'd never actually touched a piece of Lego before, and trying to fit the various blocks into a recognisable shape under the critical gazes of Holly, Tom and both the dogs proved something of a trial.

'It's all wobbly,' said Holly, when she'd finished. 'And it hasn't got a window. Why hasn't it?'

'I'm just the builder,' said Kate. 'Blame the architect.'

But Tom wasn't nearly so censorious. He sat and stared at it for a few minutes then treated Kate to another of his radiant smiles before clumping rather unsteadily across to her and planting a sticky kiss on her cheek.

It was a totally unexpected gesture, and Kate felt oddly touched by it. Neither of the children had ever been particularly demonstrative with her in the past. Indeed, she was aware that Sally had cautioned them more than once about being a nuisance to her. But there'd been something very satisfying about the trustful way Tom's sturdy little body had leaned against her. And not even the realisation that his clutching hand had left a perfect set of fingerprints on the front of her cream shirt could detract from that.

She persuaded Holly to help her build some tracks with the rest of the Lego for Tom to drive his cars down, and they were occupied with this when she heard the sound of the Mercedes coming up the drive.

'Mummy.' Holly took off joyously across the grass, as the car came to a halt, and Sally emerged from the front passenger seat, bending to greet her daughter. The men left the car more slowly, bringing the newspapers and various carrier bags.

For a moment, they all stood by the car and Kate could feel four pairs of eyes boring into her across the expanse of lawn. As she got slowly to her feet,

Tom tugged at the leg of her trousers, and held his arms out, asking mutely to be carried.

'You're supposed to walk, Tom-Tom,' Kate told him gently, using the pet name employed by the rest of the family, but she lifted him into her arms anyway, and stood holding him.

No, she amended mentally. Holding *on* to him. Because she was suddenly aware that she was shaking inside. And that she felt disturbingly—painfully self-conscious. And that the little body in her arms was a shield.

It was clear from their reactions, more wary than actually surprised, that Mrs Lassiter had indeed rung the pub to warn them of her presence. But why she should have done so was beyond Kate's comprehension.

It took all her courage to pin on some kind of smile as they moved towards her, Ryan leading the way. His eyes were hidden behind dark glasses, and the rest of his face seemed totally expressionless.

Kate, recalling the nature of their earlier parting, felt her heart sink.

'Hi,' she greeted them, trying to sound nonchalant. 'The weather was too lovely for work, so I thought I'd join you.' She saw Ben and Edward Lassiter exchange glances, and added, 'I—I hope that's all right.'

'It's fine, my dear. Couldn't be better,' her father-in-law said heartily. 'We see far too little of you. I was just saying so to Ryan earlier.'

'Oh,' said Kate, wondering whether or not Ryan had agreed with him. There was certainly no indication in his impassive expression.

Sally stepped forward, her eyes fixed on her small son who was fidgeting now that he'd seen her. 'Kate—let me take Tom. He's far too heavy for you. And he's always filthy,' she added, with a slight intake of breath as she removed him firmly from Kate's grasp. 'Just look at the mess he's made of your shirt. Oh, dear, I'm so sorry.' She shook her head at the little boy. 'Tom-Tom, I've told you not to pester Aunty Kate.'

'He wasn't pestering me,' Kate protested, swiftly. 'And the shirt will wash.'

But Sally was already carrying the child towards the house, scolding him fondly. Kate watched them go, feeling momentarily bereft, then turned back to her father-in-law with a determined smile.

'The—the garden's looking wonderful,' she ventured, hoping that it was true.

'You seem to be wearing some of it,' Ryan remarked quietly. He stepped forward, and removed a couple of beech leaves from her hair. 'How on earth did you manage that?'

'Aunty Kate was hiding in the hedge,' said Holly, emerging from under the table where she'd been ensconced with the dogs.

Ryan paused. 'Hiding in the hedge?' he repeated on a note of incredulity.

'I was looking over the gate,' nodded the child from hell. 'And I seed her.'

'Saw her,' Ben corrected her automatically, then stopped. 'At least—I'm sure you didn't, Holly. Don't tell stories.'

'I did too see her,' Holly said obstinately.

Kate, conscious that Edward Lassiter and Ben were staring at her with astonishment, glanced at Ryan, and saw his mouth twisting in faint amusement. She felt a wave of defensive colour sweep up into her face.

She said, snatching at her dignity, 'I wasn't hiding at all. I was walking round the side of the house, and I thought I heard an animal in distress—a cat.'

Mr Lassiter laughed. 'It would be a brave cat who'd come within a mile of the place, my dear. Algy and Thistle see to that. But it was a kind thought.'

'Indeed it was.' Ryan had removed his sunglasses and was studying her. 'And did you find this—afflicted creature?' he queried softly.

'I'm afraid not.' Kate dropped hurriedly to one knee on the rug, and busied herself with putting the Lego back in its tub.

'What a pity,' he murmured.

'Well, we'd better take these things indoors,' said Mr Lassiter briskly. 'It's about five minutes to lunch.'

He and Ben walked away, leaving Kate alone with Ryan. She went on packing away Lego, aware her hands were trembling.

He squatted beside her, picking up the garage, and

studying it critically. 'An interesting concept,' he commented.

'Oh, shut up.' Kate snatched it back. 'Tom liked it, anyway. And will you pass me those cars, please?'

'Speaking of which—what did you do with yours?'

'Oh, I left it round the corner somewhere.' Kate nodded vaguely in the general direction.

'So that you could hunt for more stray animals on the way, perhaps?' He shook his head. 'I never knew you were so interested in flora and fauna, darling. It's given me a whole new insight into your personality.'

She lifted her head and looked at him. 'Isn't that what marriage is all about?' she asked deliberately. 'Two people changing—developing side by side?'

Ryan's smile did not reach his eyes. 'I don't know, my sweet,' he drawled. 'You tell me.' He put the toy cars into a neat pile, and stood up, dusting his hands on his chinos. 'Now, let's go and eat.'

He reached down and pulled Kate to her feet, his hands firm on her shoulders, sending ripples of awareness tingling through her body.

He looked down at her, his eyes lingering on her parted lips. She looked back at him mutely, feeling her breathing quicken, waiting for him to bend his head and kiss her. Needing the reassurance of his mouth on hers.

He said gently, 'I hope you've got an appetite,' then let her go, and walked away over the grass towards the house.

Kate stood watching his retreat. The sun poured

down on her in dazzling warmth, but she felt chilled to the very bone.

Coming here had clearly been a big mistake, she thought, swallowing. And at the moment she wasn't at all sure how to retrieve the situation. Or even—if she could do so.

And she knew suddenly that she was more deeply, shakingly afraid than she had ever been in her life.

CHAPTER FOUR

'I've been looking at the sample menus from this new catering firm,' announced Louie. 'Darling, they're bland to the point of being invisible. Surely you aren't going to use them? Are you, Kate?' She snapped her fingers. 'Hey, have you gone into a trance?'

Kate, who'd been staring unseeingly at the page of figures in front of her, jumped guiltily.

'I'm sorry, Lou. I—I was thinking about something else. What were you saying?'

'These menus, love.' Louie gave the papers in her hand a disparaging look. 'Supreme of chicken in mushroom sauce—minted lamb chops—beef casserole. Are we awarding prizes for originality here?'

Kate sighed. 'I thought I might use them for this retirement dinner next month. According to his wife, the guest of honour has a funny tummy, and only likes plain food.'

'There's plain, and there's downright ugly,' Louie grumbled. 'We do have our reputation to consider.' She patted Kate on the shoulder. 'But you know best.'

Do I? thought Kate, bitterly. I wonder.

She said quietly, 'I suggest we try them once, and see how it goes.'

She looked up to find Louie giving her a narrow look over the top of her glasses.

'You look, my dear, as if you've been washed, wrung out, and drip-dried.' She winked, naughtily. 'Sleepless night, you lucky girl?'

Kate flushed slightly. 'No, nothing like that,' she said with constraint. You couldn't be further from the truth, she added silently, suppressing a wince.

She forced a smile. 'Actually, I think I spent too long in the sun yesterday, and it's given me a slight headache.'

Louie looked surprised. 'I thought you were the original lizard. Drape you over a rock, and let you sizzle gently all day.'

'Not any more, apparently,' Kate returned, transferring her attention determinedly back to her work.

But Louie lingered. 'Are you sure you're all right?' she persisted. 'You look like a woman with problems.'

Silently, Kate damned her friend's perception. She was sorely tempted to pour out the whole story, starting with the anonymous letter, but something held her back, warning her that once the genie had escaped from the bottle it would never be possible to confine it again. That a confidence, once given, could never be retracted, and that a time might come when she would wish every word unsaid.

If there was a crisis in her marriage, it was something she should deal with alone—unless it reached a stage where it was impossible to hide the truth any longer.

If Ryan left her, for example, she thought, feeling slow pain twist inside her.

She pulled an exaggerated face. 'Can't fool you, babe. I put myself through Sunday lunch with the in-laws yesterday. I'm still recovering.'

Louie frowned. 'I thought you liked them.'

'I do—really. But that doesn't stop me feeling like an outsider looking in when I'm in their company for any length of time.' Kate was astonished at the depth of feeling in her voice. She was conscious of the previous day, hanging over her like a shadow. And the previous night.

'Does Ryan know how you feel?'

Kate shrugged defensively. 'Ryan and I seem to be having slight communication problems at the moment.' She managed a brittle laugh. 'I gather these are normal, and that all the best marriages have them.'

'Well, you certainly have one of the best marriages,' Louie told her levelly. 'So you should know. But I'd make sure it's only a temporary hiccup.'

And, with another, more admonitory pat, she departed.

As the door closed behind her, Kate slumped back in her high-backed leather chair, twisting her pen restlessly in her fingers.

It was good advice, she thought, if only it was possible to take it. But how could she communicate with someone who'd apparently surrounded himself with a wall of glass, leaving her to batter herself against it fruitlessly, time after time?

It wasn't as if he'd quarrelled with her, or even been dismissive. He hadn't told her that she'd had no business to follow him, or made any hurtful remark, for that matter. He'd simply been, in some strange way—unreachable.

She wished with all her heart that she hadn't gone down to Whitmead after all. The whole day had been an unmitigated disaster. The food, as usual, had been delicious, but Kate had felt she was chewing cardboard and sawdust. And there were so many awkwardnesses and embarrassed silences that she'd almost lost count. Once, as she'd entered the sitting room, she'd interrupted a low-voiced conversation between Mrs Lassiter and Sally which had ceased abruptly the moment she'd appeared.

As if they all knew something that I didn't—and certainly weren't prepared to discuss it in front of me, she told herself miserably.

As indeed they might have been, she had to admit. Ryan was close to his parents and always had been. He wouldn't have her misgivings about sharing his problems.

Perhaps if her own mother were near at hand, instead of living in Spain with her second husband, she would do the same.

Kate bit her lip. No, she thought sadly. No, I wouldn't. Mother and I have never had that kind of relationship. We were always too busy trying to keep our heads above water financially.

A mixture of pride and bravado had kept her at Whitmead until early evening. She'd left just after Ryan himself, but hadn't taken the direct route back to London. She'd told herself she had too much to think about, but in her heart she'd known the real reason was that she didn't want to arrive back home at the empty flat.

As she'd driven, she'd decided that things could not go on as they were. That she had to confront Ryan, and demand the truth, no matter how painful the result might be.

When she'd got home, a gleam of light under the closed study door had told her that Ryan was in there, presumably working.

Or simply keeping me at bay, she'd thought miserably. She'd toyed with the idea of marching in there, and demanding to know what was going on, but the habit of leaving him in peace was too strong.

Or was it rock-bottom cowardice? she asked herself now, defeatedly. Was she afraid to ask the question in case she couldn't live with the answer?

When he'd finally emerged, she was sitting apparently engrossed in a television programme.

'Any good?'

'Total rubbish,' she lied, not wanting to admit she hadn't absorbed one word or one image. She got to her feet. 'I've made a Waldorf salad for supper. Would you like hot French bread with it?'

'It sounds too good to be true.' Ryan sat down and became immediately absorbed in the television.

'Did I tell you that Quentin thinks the last book is going to be made into a mini-series?' he said, as she came back with a tray.

She gasped. 'Darling—that's marvellous news. Or isn't it?' she added, seeing his ironic smile.

'I think it's too early to say. It rather depends how they hack it around, and who gets to play the lead. Quentin says I should take the money and run, but I'd like to retain a vestige of artistic control, if I can.'

'Well, I still think it's terrific. We should celebrate.' Kate paused, about to place a foot squarely on thin ice. 'Have we got any champagne?' Her tone was almost too casual.

There was a pause, then he said, 'I wouldn't think so for a moment. But there's rather a good Pomerol I've been waiting to open. Will that do instead?'

She wanted to say, But you do drink champagne sometimes—don't you? But she didn't dare. And what kind of fool did that make her?

Instead, 'Yes,' she agreed, tonelessly. 'Yes, of course, the Pomerol will be fine.'

When the wine was poured, she raised her glass to him in a toast. 'Here's to our side.' She paused. 'Did Quentin phone this evening? Surely not.'

'No,' he said. 'I've known for a few days.'

She stared at him. 'And you didn't bother to tell me.'

He shrugged. 'We've both been pretty occupied.'

'Well, thanks for remembering me at last.' Her voice rose a notch.

'You're welcome.' He smiled at her, totally unfazed. 'Did I ever tell you that you make the best Waldorf salad in the world?'

'Once or twice.' She put down her fork. 'Ryan—don't shut me out.'

The words were instinctive, forced from her. And if he made some joke back she would probably die.

But his face was totally serious. 'Is that what I'm doing?'

You tell me. Aloud, she said, 'I—I don't know. We just don't seem to have the same amount of time for each other any more.'

He said drily, 'We're not still honeymooners. And our lives have changed. We both have demanding jobs.'

She played with the stem of her glass. 'Couldn't we have a second honeymoon?'

'Back to Bordeaux to buy some more wine?'

'Not necessarily. And I didn't know that had been the main purpose of the exercise, anyway.' She paused. 'I thought—an island, somewhere.'

He was silent for a moment. 'I'm fully tied up for some time ahead. Maybe we could manage a few days in the autumn.'

'Maybe.' Her smile was taut. 'We'll compare diaries.'

But that's not what I want, she thought, picking at her salad. I want you to fling a couple of air tickets at me, and tell me to pack a bikini and a dress and forget my underwear.

I want us to say to hell with deadlines and clients, and just—take off together like we used to.

But you could never go back, she thought. Only forward.

There was a time when she'd seen their future together like a straight and shining path on which they walked side by side. Now, it seemed to be turning into parallel lines.

She collected their plates together. 'There's cheese and fruit.'

'Nothing more for me, thanks.' He smiled at her.

'Are you going to work tonight?' She saw his brows lift and hurried on. 'Because I thought we could put on some music. It's ages since we've done that.'

It's ages since we've done a lot of things.

'Okay,' Ryan agreed. 'But with a few pre-conditions.' He ticked them off on his fingers. 'We choose turn and turn about, and we don't whinge at the other one's selection, or talk through it, or fall asleep...'

'I did that once,' Kate said indignantly. 'And just for that I'll pick first.'

She made her own selections carefully, choosing pieces that had some special, intimate meaning for them both. Willing him silently to remember, as she sat beside him on one of the sofas. She was intensely conscious of his relaxed, graceful body stretched out beside her. She wanted him to reach out and pull her close, pillowing her head on his shoulder.

But he stayed as he was, his arms crossed behind his head.

Her last choice was, she thought, inspired. It was one of the first compact discs they'd bought while they were living at the old flat. Rachmaninov's Variations on a Theme by Paganini, and they'd made sweet, soaring love on the rug in front of the fire while the glorious, romantic sweep of the Eighteenth variation filled the room.

He couldn't have forgotten, surely, she thought, stealing a sideways glance at him from under her lashes.

Only to catch him smothering a yawn.

He grinned at her apologetically. 'Sorry, darling, but I'm bushed. That fencing of Dad's was too much like hard work.'

She hid her disappointment, smiling determinedly back at him. 'Well, you go to bed, and I'll clear up down here.'

When she went up to bed, he was lying on his side reading.

Not asleep, she noted exultantly. Waiting for her, perhaps?

She undressed in the bathroom. She didn't bother with the ivory nightgown. Instead, she just touched her pulse spots with Patou's Joy.

When she returned to the bedroom, Ryan had put down his book, and extinguished his lamp.

So far, so good, Kate thought, as she slid into bed, and snuggled up to him, her bare breasts pressed against his naked back, one hand sliding coaxingly over his smooth flank.

'Rub my back for me, Katie?'

He hadn't called her that for a while, Kate thought triumphantly, as she reached into the drawer of her night table for the small bottle of scented oil she always used. She knelt beside him, pouring a little of the oil into her cupped hands. She applied it lightly to his back, then began to work, her palms sweeping up the length of his spine to the nape of his neck, and across his shoulders, her fingers firm on the knotted muscles. Listening to his murmur of pleasure and contentment as she repeated the movement over and over again, finding the tension points and loosening them.

Kate herself was far from immune from what she was doing. The sensation of his skin under her hands carried a deeply erotic charge. She was aware of her nipples hardening. Of the delicious, sensuous ache in the very core of her womanhood.

She bent her head, and slowly retraced the path her hands had taken, this time with her lips. She nibbled tiny kisses up his neck, and tugged gently at his earlobe with her teeth.

She said softly, 'Why don't you turn over, and let me cure all your aching muscles?'

And waited for him to roll on to his back, and pull her down to him, sheathing himself in the moist darkness of her body with a groan of satisfaction.

Only he didn't move. And his breath wasn't ragged with newly kindled desire, but smooth and even.

My God, Kate thought, torn between anger and sheer physical frustration. I don't believe it. I've sent him to sleep.

I was a damn sight kinder to him than I was to myself, she thought now, staring at the screen of her computer. As it was she'd tossed and turned for most of the night, furiously aware of Ryan's untroubled slumber beside her.

She'd slept eventually, only to be awoken by the sound of the shower, and Ryan's cheerful whistling from the bathroom. As if, she thought vengefully, he didn't have a care in the world.

In the past, a back massage had always been a big turn-on for him. He'd never before failed to respond to her ministrations.

A pattern seemed to be emerging in their relationship that she did not even dare to contemplate.

He'd emerged from the bathroom, towelling his hair dry, his only covering another towel draped loosely round his hips.

'Morning, Katie.' His grin had been as casual as his greeting. 'Sleep well?'

'You clearly did.' She couldn't hide the note of acid in her voice, but Ryan had appeared not to notice.

'I told you I was bushed.' He'd combed his damp hair into place, then dropped the towel he was wearing to the floor as he reached for a pair of the brief black underpants he favoured. 'And you have healing hands, my love.'

Not sexy hands. Not arousing hands, but healing hands. Good old Nurse Katie, she thought furiously. She sounded like some lovable character from a day-time soap.

She'd said coolly, 'Thank you—I think,' then had tossed back the covers and got out of bed. She'd never been self-conscious about being naked in front of Ryan in the past, but as she'd walked past him to the bathroom today every inch of her had seemed to be burning up.

But that was what a man's indifference did to you, she thought wretchedly, re-living every step. You felt you had to cover up, and tiptoe.

But how long could she go on like this?

At midday, she telephoned the apartment, to suggest that Ryan meet her somewhere for lunch, but the answering machine was on, and she rang off without leaving a message.

He might be working, and not wish to be disturbed. Or he might be out somewhere with—someone. And, somehow, she didn't want to know.

In spite of her heavy thoughts, she managed to get through her day's work, although she knew that, for once, she hadn't given it her best shot.

She was just finishing a quote for a silver wedding, when Louie came breezing in. 'Know any authentic Greek restaurants? Guy wants to take his wife out for an anniversary dinner as near to their honeymoon on

Corfu as he can get. All retsina, smashing plates and lukewarm chips.'

'Why doesn't he just take her back to Corfu?' Kate said dourly.

'That's not the attitude,' Louie reproved. 'We're Special Occasions, remember?'

Kate sighed. 'I know—and I'm sorry. I'll give it some thought tonight.'

Louie gave her a long look. 'Why not let tonight start now?' she suggested. 'You've been really quiet all day. It might do you good to go home early. Devote some time to Ryan. Hell, have your very own Special Occasion.'

'Perhaps,' Kate said slowly, 'that's not such a bad idea.'

She'd play it cool, she told herself on the way home. No more heavy-handed attempts at seduction, which only ended in her own humiliation and frustration. Instead, she'd try and re-open the lines of communication. Find out if there was anything left.

And if there wasn't? she asked herself, desperately. What then? What could she do—how could she survive?

She shook her head in disbelief. Only forty-eight hours ago, she'd been totally in control. I was the business, she thought. But now I'm running round like a headless chicken. And it can't go on, whatever the consequences.

The apartment was quiet when she let herself in,

but Ryan's office door was shut, indicating that he was in there working.

Normally, she wouldn't have interrupted him, but there was nothing normal about the present circumstances, she thought wryly as she reached for the door handle, only to pause as she heard him speak.

He was obviously talking on the telephone, not loudly, but the door's panels were thin, and she was standing too close to avoid overhearing what he was saying.

'No.' His voice was clear, reassuring. 'She has no idea, I swear it.' A brief silence, then, 'Yes, of course it's only a matter of time before she realises, but we'll deal with that when we need to. And you mustn't worry about it. It's my problem. Bye, sweetheart.' And the phone went down.

Kate stood, her hand still extended towards the door handle, as if she'd been turned to stone. Eavesdroppers, she thought numbly. What was that old saying about eavesdroppers? That they never heard anything to their own advantage. And, like so many clichés, it held a hard and bitter kernel of truth.

She wanted to tear down the door with her nails. She wanted to scream and rave, and batter him with her fists. Ryan, her husband—her betrayer.

But she did none of those things. Instead of opening the door and walking straight in, she knocked quietly, and waited.

The door was flung open, and Ryan looked her over, his brows caught together in a faint frown.

He said courteously, but coldly, 'I hope this is important.'

She wanted to say, You mean as important as the conversation you've just been having? But panic held her mute. She swallowed, searching for the right words, and was suddenly aware of an intense feeling of nausea.

'Kate.' There was a thinly veiled note of impatience in his voice. 'What is it?' His frown deepened as he surveyed her. 'Is something wrong?'

That was the moment, of course. The moment to say, Yes, I know that you're in love with someone else, and it's crucifying me.

Instead, she said hoarsely, 'I—I think I'm going to be sick.'

She gagged, then covered her mouth, and ran, half stumbling, up to the bathroom.

The ten minutes which followed were painful and unpleasant, and left her totally drained, her head swimming.

She hadn't even realised that Ryan had followed her, until he came to kneel beside her, cradling her head against his shoulder, and wiping her face with a wet cloth.

'Thank you,' she managed.

'Hush,' he said quietly. 'There's no need to say anything.' He helped her to her feet, and out of the bathroom.

He sat her down on the edge of the bed, removed her shoes, then began to unbutton her shirt. His fingers were gentle but totally impersonal, and that, Kate realised, feeling the first scalding tear on her cheek, was somehow the worst thing of all. The ultimate confirmation of the nightmare.

'I can manage.' Some remnant of pride forced the words from her in an agonised croak.

'I'm sure you can,' he agreed levelly. 'But I intend to help, just the same.'

He undressed her as if she were a child, slipped the ivory nightgown over her head, then turned back the covers and lifted her into bed.

He said, 'And there's no need to cry, either.'

She thought, Isn't there? *Isn't there?*

Aloud, she said, 'I know.' She reached for a box of tissues. 'I just hate being sick, that's all.'

'I see.' He was silent for a moment, then said, 'I'd better ring my mother—find out if anyone else has been ill.'

'Oh, no.' She caught at his sleeve. 'I—I'm sure it was nothing I ate. I mean—you're obviously fine and I—well, I haven't really been feeling well all day.'

His brows lifted. 'I see. Is that why you came home early?'

Kate touched the scalloped edge of the sheet, avoiding his gaze. 'One of the reasons.'

'It was quite a surprise,' he said drily.

And for me, she thought. And for me. My life has been teeming with them just lately.

She said, 'I—I wish it had been a more pleasant surprise.' She drew a breath. 'For both of us.'

There was another taut silence, then he said, 'Would you like some brandy?'

She shook her head. 'Just a glass of spring water, please. There's some in the fridge.'

She watched him go downstairs, then reached across to her night table for a handmirror. She winced when she saw herself—white-faced, hollow-eyed with her hair hanging in damp, lank strands.

What a pitiful-looking object, she thought with self-disgust.

If she asked Ryan for the truth now, he might hedge, because he felt sorry for her, and wanted to spare her. To let her down lightly, if that was possible under the present circumstances.

And I don't need sympathy, she told herself, putting the mirror back in the drawer. I need to know. But I also want to be on my feet, and strong, able to fight my corner.

Unless the prospect of losing him was always going to have the same dire physical affect on her, she thought wryly. She now knew the meaning of the words 'sick with fright'.

When Ryan returned with her water, she thanked him stiltedly, and sipped it, aware of his scrutiny.

He said abruptly, 'You were ill a few weeks ago, as well. I think you should see a doctor.'

'I'm sure there's no need,' Kate said quickly. 'It was just a tummy bug, last time. Louie got it as well.'

'And this time?'

'Probably the same kind of thing,' she dismissed. 'Anyway, I feel much better now. Fine, in fact.'

His smile held a faint grimness. 'You look like a ghost. I suggest you get some sleep.'

She said quietly, 'You're probably right.' She drank some more water. 'Are you—going back to work?'

'I have to.' He didn't sound particularly regretful. 'But I'll try not to wake you when I come up. And if you start to feel ill again, call me.'

As he turned away, she thought frantically, Don't leave me. Don't go.

She said, 'Ryan,' her voice breathless, and he paused at the head of the stairs, his brows lifting enquiringly.

'Is something wrong?'

Kate's courage failed her. She said, 'I just wanted to say—thanks for looking after me.'

She saw a glimpse of his crooked smile. 'It's part of the marriage service, isn't it?' He quoted softly, '"For better for worse... In sickness and in health..."'

She shook her head, forcing a smile that was more like a grimace. 'I don't think they included that—at the registry office.'

He said quietly, 'Perhaps they should have done.' And went downstairs.

Kate lay back against her pillows and closed her eyes, staring into a deeper darkness than she had ever experienced.

And what about 'till death us do part'? she wondered bleakly, her throat tightening. Had that been a deliberate omission?

She supposed the proud, brave thing to do would be to offer Ryan his freedom, but she didn't feel proud, or brave.

She felt frightened, and confused, and—yes—incredulous. Was it possible that she'd simply allowed their brief marriage to wither and die, totally unaware? That Ryan had ceased, at some point, to be her lover, her friend, her companion, and she hadn't noticed?

What she did know was that she was not prepared to hand him over to some unknown woman. Not without a fight.

Know your enemy, she thought. That was what she needed to do. To somehow find out her rival's identity, see what she was up against, and then go to work.

The anonymous letter must have come from the other woman. There was no other explanation, and if 'X' was prepared to take that kind of risk maybe she wasn't too sure of her own position. Perhaps this was her way of forcing the issue. And, of course, she'd been keen to know Kate's reaction, wanting, no doubt, to hear about murder, mayhem, banged doors and divorce proceedings.

Ryan's reassurances, just now, must have been really bad news for her. She'd be on tenterhooks, wondering now if Kate had even got the letter.

And she can stay there too, Kate thought vengefully. Let her worry, and walk the floor. Sending that letter could have been a really stupid move, because it's put me on her trail. And if she wants mayhem, I'm quite prepared to give it to her. When I find her.

And, with that, she turned on her side, and to her own surprise fell deeply and dreamlessly asleep.

CHAPTER FIVE

WHEN she awoke, it was morning, but there was nothing about the way the light fell across the bedroom floor which told her it was much later than usual. A glance at her clock confirmed this.

'Oh, God.' She pushed back the covers, and almost fell out of bed, grabbing her robe. She launched herself down the stairs.

Ryan was standing by one of the living-room windows, coffee mug in hand. He turned as she hurtled into view, his brows lifting.

'What's the rush?'

'I'm horrendously late,' Kate threw over her shoulder as she went into the kitchen. 'I must have slept through the alarm.'

'Actually, I turned it off.' He followed, and stood watching as she flicked the switch to re-boil the kettle, threw a tea bag into a beaker, and began to hack at a lemon. 'Here, let me do that.' He strolled forward and took the knife from her hand.

'Why?'

'Because you're still half asleep, and I don't want you to cut your wrist instead of the lemon.' His mouth twisted ironically. 'Besides, bleeding all over the units could damage our property values.'

'Not that,' Kate dismissed impatiently. 'Why did you turn off my alarm?'

'You seemed to need your sleep.' Ryan added the lemon slice to the tea bag, and covered both with boiling water. 'And, as you were sick yesterday, I thought you might want to take today off, anyway.'

Her heart skipped a beat. 'Do you think I should?'

'I'd say that's your decision.' He turned and gave her a long look. 'You know how you feel.'

'Mmm.' She fidgeted with a spoon, glancing at him sideways, from under her lashes. 'But don't you prefer the flat to yourself when you're working?'

'Actually, I shan't be here.' Ryan discarded the tea bag, and handed her the fragrant-smelling beaker, which could have contained dishwater for all her interest in it.

'I see.' Kate made an elaborate business of taking a cautious sip. 'Doing anything interesting?'

Trying to sound pleasantly casual, when she wanted to knock him to the floor and torture the truth out of him with lighted cigarettes, was not easy, she decided grimly.

'This and that.' He rinsed out his empty mug, and stood it in the drying-rack.

Did this bitch realise what a house-trained paragon she was getting? Kate wondered furiously.

'Later on I'm having lunch with my editor,' he went on.

'Oh.' Kate relaxed ever so slightly. He wouldn't stray very far with Joe Hartley, who'd been his editor

ever since he joined Chatsworth Blair. Joe was a relaxed, humorous, razor-witted guy, with a wife he
adored. Ryan needn't think he'd find any sympathy in
that quarter. Joe would be far more likely to bawl him
out, to make him see what he was throwing away.

'That's terrific,' she continued, with genuine
warmth. 'How is old Joe?'

Ryan paused. Then, 'He's fine.'

Kate thought she detected an odd note in his voice,
and looked at him swiftly, but he looked calm, even
slightly smiling, and this emboldened her.

'Tell you what,' she said. 'I'm not doing anything
for lunch today. Why don't I join you? It's ages since
I've seen him.'

'Not this time, darling,' Ryan said pleasantly. 'It's
a strictly editorial lunch. I'm handing over the first
draft of the new book, and we'll be discussing that
rather than social niceties. And you know how bored
you get with literary chat.'

Kate flushed, and took another sip of lemon tea.
'That's not true,' she protested. 'I take enormous interest in your work.'

'Yes, when it's wearing a jacket and on sale in
Harrods.' His smile took any sting from the words.
'But you're not too enamoured by all the mysterious
processes that get the words on to the paper. Admit
it.'

'Perhaps not,' she said slowly. 'But that's because
they take you away from me.'

It wasn't what she'd meant to say at all. She hadn't even been aware of the thought formulating.

'I'm here, Kate.' Ryan's voice was soft, and oddly intense. 'I've always been here. Writing is a solitary craft. You're the one who goes out to work, who meets the people, and does the deals.'

What was he trying to tell her? she asked herself, with a sudden stab of desolation. That even when he'd gone she would still have a life—of sorts?

She shivered, pulling a condemnatory face at the inoffensive lemon tea. 'And if I don't get cracking there won't be any deals.'

He was watching her again. 'Sure you feel up to it?'

'Fighting fit.' She sounded bright enough to dazzle. 'Is the bathroom free?'

'It's all yours.' He ran a hand round his chin. 'I shaved after I had my shower.'

On impulse, she put down her beaker and went towards him, reaching up on tiptoe. 'Let me sniff.' She kept her voice light.

It was one of the small jokey intimacies they'd always shared, this gentle inhalation of the scent of his skin, so familiar to her that if she'd been presented, blindfold, with a hundred other men, she would pick him without hesitation.

From their earliest time together, it had filled her with delight.

'Oh, God.' She could remember nuzzling him, nipping him softly with her teeth, unable to get enough of him. 'You smell wonderful.'

And him turning to her, gathering her up in his arms, his hands urgent, his voice husky. 'And so do you, Kate—*Katie*...'

Often—so often—this tiny nonsense had led to them falling back into bed together, uncaring of the time, or other obligations. Oblivious, indeed, to everything but their mutual need, and its heated, ecstatic fulfilment.

No one's marriage could survive at that pitch for ever, Kate reminded herself. But it would do no harm to remind him of what they'd had together. And what they could still have.

She breathed deeply, burying her nose in his lean cheek, even as her senses alerted her sharply to a difference.

She stepped back. 'You've changed your cologne.'

'Yes, it's one I bought at the airport on the last trip. Do you like it?'

'I—I don't know.' Nor did she. It was much lighter and more floral than the usual one. Did *she*—'X', the unknown quantity—like it? she wondered.

She said hurriedly, 'Perhaps it's a bit young.'

His grin was sardonic. 'Aren't you the flatterer? Go and dress while I polish my Zimmer frame.'

She flushed. 'I didn't mean that as it sounded. It just doesn't seem to be—you.'

'Ah,' he said lightly. 'But perhaps this is the beginning of a whole new me.'

Yes, Kate thought, as she trailed back upstairs. That's what I'm afraid of.

On the other hand, maybe she was too much the same, she thought as she surveyed herself, dressed and ready for another working day. The brief navy skirt, the immaculate silk blouse, the scarlet double-breasted blazer were almost like a uniform. She wore a similar version of the same thing every day. Not too formal for the office, but smart enough to take her to meetings with clients. But not bloody exciting, that was for sure.

She hardly thought Ryan's eyes would light up when he saw her.

And she was right, because when she got downstairs he was talking on the telephone, and didn't even notice her.

'Fine,' he was saying briskly. 'One o'clock. I'm looking forward to it.' He replaced the receiver, wrote something swiftly on the pad next to the phone, tore off the sheet, and stuffed it into his pocket.

'Chatsworth Blair?' She gave him an enquiring glance.

He nodded, his expression already preoccupied, going ahead of her into the solitary world he inhabited where she could not follow. 'Confirming lunch.'

He picked up his briefcase, and headed for the door. 'I'll see you later.'

'Have a good day,' she called after him. 'Give my love to Joe.'

But he was already closing the door, and didn't seem to have heard her.

Kate collected her own briefcase and bag, and went over to switch on the answering machine. She stood for a moment, looking down at the blank pad. There'd been a scene in a film she'd enjoyed—something by Hitchcock and Cary Grant—where he'd read a message he wasn't supposed to see, simply by running a pencil over the indentations in the next sheet of paper.

Almost idly, as if acting outside her own volition, Kate picked up the pencil, and brushed the lead over the marks on the pad.

'Amaryllis,' she read aloud, then paused, frowning.

But that's the new restaurant that opened in Denbigh Street a week or two ago, she thought, puzzled. And Joe Hartley always takes Ryan to Scotts, because they both love fish. It's like a ritual for them.

Slowly, she tore the sheet from the pad, and stowed it in her bag.

Everything seemed to be changing, she thought, from the vitally important to the relatively trivial. She felt like a child, robbed of its security blanket, and she didn't like it.

It was an edgy morning altogether. Kate was dreading an interrogation from Louie on how the previous evening had gone, but—perhaps fortunately—her partner was dealing with the crisis of a last-minute replacement for their favourite florist, who'd broken her wrist and would be unable to undertake the promised arrangements for a looming wedding.

Kate completed a couple of quotations, dealt with a letter from a disgruntled client, convinced that inferior sherry had been served at his daughter's reception, and finalised the menu to be served at the celebration lunch for a venerable detective novelist's fiftieth book.

But at the same time her mind was churning, reviewing everything that had happened, and finding little for her comfort.

She was particularly concerned over Ryan's reason for turning down her company at lunch. Did he really think she was uninterested in his work? she wondered, chewing the end of an inoffensive pen.

I don't altogether understand it, and I may resent it, she told herself honestly, but it doesn't bore me.

But could this have driven the first wedge between them, and rendered him prey to this other relationship? she asked herself uneasily. Did 'X' sit at his feet, perhaps, reading every word and offering helpful critiques? Was this how she'd got to him?

It was Debbie, the PA, putting her head round the door to ask if Kate wanted the usual sandwiches for lunch that brought her to an abrupt decision.

'No, thanks, I'm going out. And could you bring in the folder with the reviews on new restaurants, Debs?'

I'll go and join them, she thought. I've always got on with Joe, and we can have one of our mock flirtations—make Ryan see me as a woman again. And show him that I do care about what he does. I'll knock him sideways with my intelligent interest.

She read what the critics had to say about the Amaryllis twice. No minimalist chic here, it seemed. 'Luscious French cooking, and decor to match,' was one quote. 'Lots of red velvet and discreetly intimate booths,' said another, adding, 'A kind of gastronomic bordello.'

'Is it, indeed?' Kate muttered under her breath. It didn't sound the likeliest place to hand over a manuscript either. And it clearly called for something other than her neat but not gaudy office gear.

Her favourite boutique came up with the very thing, a clinging jersey dress the color of warm honey, with a deep V-neckline, tiny sleeves and a skirt flaring from mid-thigh, and slashed for extra swing. Kate added bronze pumps and a matching clutch purse and bundled her workaday clothes into a carrier for collection later.

She got the cab-driver to drop her at the end of Denbigh Street. As she walked slowly towards the restaurant, a workman painting a shopfront whistled at her—a politically incorrect move on his part which, nevertheless, warmed the cockles of Kate's unhappy heart.

The Amaryllis didn't simply protect the privacy of its clientele with red velvet. The smoked-glass windows were guarded by a small rainforest of green plants in vast ceramic tubs.

Kate, under cover of reading the selection of fixed-price menus displayed outside, tried to make a preliminary reconnaissance by peering between the fronds, but had to give it up as a bad job.

'Can I help you, *madame*?'

Kate, startled by the unseen approach of the head waiter, jumped so violently that the heavy wrought-iron stand holding the menus began to rock.

'I'm so sorry,' she muttered, appalled, as they steadied it between them. It wasn't the cool, understated entrance she'd planned. 'I'd like to have lunch.'

The waiter spread his hands. 'I much regret, *madame*, but we are fully booked. Perhaps you would like to make a reservation for another time.'

His tone was not over-effusive, suggesting that after her performance with the menu stand he could visualise her clumping through the place, wreaking havoc on the red velvet drapes, and anything else that stood in her way.

Kate bit her lip. 'Actually, I'm joining my husband,' she said with an attempt at crispness.

'Ah, yes, and his name, *madame*?'

'I think the booking will have been made by Chatsworth Blair.'

The waiter consulted a book as large as a family bible, and shook his head. 'Alas, we have no reservation in that name.'

Kate, who'd followed him into the shadowy interior, said, 'Well—Joe Hartley, then.'

'Nor for a Mr Hartley, either, *madame*.' He spoke

with a certain quiet satisfaction, the fixtures and fittings safely preserved. 'Perhaps you have mistaken the restaurant.'

'I have not,' Kate said glacially, 'mistaken the restaurant. Or the day, or the time,' she added swiftly, forestalling him. 'Perhaps I could have a quick look round—see if I can spot them.'

They certainly weren't at any of the white-clothed tables in the centre of the big room, but the velvet-festooned booths around the side were less easy to investigate.

The waiter recoiled as if she'd suggested organizing a cockroach hunt in the kitchens.

'Of what point, *madame*, when I have already told you that your husband Monsieur Hartley is not here?'

'My husband's name is not Hartley,' Kate said, flushing slightly as the waiter cast his eyes to heaven. 'It's Lassiter.'

There was a pause. Then the waiter said with clear reluctance, 'We do have a booking in that name, *madame*, but the reservation was for two persons, and his guest has already joined him.'

'Fine,' Kate said evenly. 'Please take me to them.'

For a moment, she thought he was going to refuse. She took a determined step forward, and saw him shrug, almost fatalistically, before leading the way to a booth at the far end of the room.

She'd intended to say 'Surprise, surprise' or something equally bright and crass to get her over the initial embarrassment of gatecrashing their lunch.

But that was before she saw that Ryan's lunch companion was not the stocky, dark-haired figure of Joe Hartley, but a stunning redhead in a little black dress, her flowing pre-Raphaelite tresses practically brushing his shoulder as she leaned towards him, smiling and pointing out something on the menu.

She had good teeth, too, Kate noticed detachedly. Which was a pity since they were about to be knocked down her throat.

She was shaken by the white-hot flame of rage which engulfed her. And by the pain, too.

She couldn't pretend any more that this could all be a terrible mistake, or even a bad dream. The living proof was right in front of her, and looking up as if butter wouldn't melt in her mouth.

'Kate.' Ryan got to his feet. He was looking totally composed. Not a trace of guilt anywhere, she realised incredulously. 'So you decided to join us, after all.'

He sounded almost amused, she thought with fury. As if he'd been expecting her to turn up.

Had that been his intention, all along? Had he laid a deliberate trail, meaning her to follow him here for the ultimate confrontation, because he thought she wouldn't make a scene in public? Well, he was about to discover his mistake.

'Yes,' she returned, her voice shaking a little. 'But I can see I'm intruding.'

'Not at all. I'll have the waiter bring another chair.'

Kate shook her head. 'Oh, no, darling.' She gave a brittle laugh. 'I wouldn't dream of spoiling a beautiful friendship. And anyway, I have to find someone to change the locks—always supposing you did plan to come home tonight.' Her voice had risen slightly, and she was aware of curious looks from other tables. Of the head waiter hovering, looking apprehensive.

Ryan's hand closed round her wrist. 'On the contrary,' he said between his teeth. 'You will sit down, before Penny concludes I'm married to a certifiable lunatic.'

'Do you think I give a damn what your—Penny thinks?' A bright spot of colour burning in either cheek, Kate tried to release herself. 'I gather she's a writer too—although she prefers writing letters to novels.'

'That's her job.' His tone was blunt. 'And I think you should pay heed to her opinion. You could be seeing a fair bit of her over the coming year while Joe's in New York.'

'What the hell are you talking about?' Kate tried to keep the aggression going, but her legs felt suddenly wobbly, and she was quite glad to sit down on the chair brought by the watchful waiter.

'I'm Penny Barnes, Mrs Lassiter.' The redhead, looking wary, stretched out a polite hand to be shaken across the table. 'I've taken over as your husband's editor at Chatsworth Blair during Joe's absence.'

'Oh, really?' Kate ignored the conciliatory gesture. 'I suppose that's why he told me he was meeting Joe today.'

'Actually, I didn't,' Ryan said quietly, re-seating

himself. 'That was all your own idea. I told you three months ago that Joe was being transferred to the New York office for a year.'

She stared at him. 'I don't remember anything of the kind.'

'Probably not.' He looked at her dispassionately. 'You were far more interested in a contract you'd just landed for some Sloane Ranger's wedding. I felt at the time you hadn't listened to a word I'd said.' He watched the colour drain out of her face, and signalled to the waiter. 'Would you bring my wife some still mineral water, please? And hold back our order until she's had a chance to look at a menu,' he added.

Kate's mouth felt as dry as a desert. She shook her head numbly, not daring to look at Penny Barnes. 'I— I'm not hungry.'

'Of course you are.' His tone brooked no further argument. Her role now, she understood, was to sit still and behave herself. And there wasn't a thing she could do about it. Not now she'd made herself into the fool of the century.

A huge starched napkin was laid reverently across her lap, making retreat well-nigh impossible anyway. She looked at the cutlery being laid before her, and wondered if any of the knives were sharp enough to cut her throat.

Ryan was ordering for her. 'Madame will have *boudin noir* with apples, followed by a *filet mignon* and a green salad.'

And a side order of cyanide, thought Kate.

The lunch proceeded, with no further reference to Kate's *faux pas*. Penny Barnes was clearly charming, intelligent and efficient. She and Ryan were discussing points in the story outline he'd originally submitted that Joe had thought might prove problematic, and he was explaining how he'd dealt with them.

At any other time, Kate would have found the conversation fascinating. A glimpse into a world she needed to understand. A world she used to be part of, she realised with a sense of shock.

Now, she simply felt sick to her stomach, pushing the unwanted food round her plate and trying to hide it under a friendly lettuce leaf.

Looking back, she could indeed recall Ryan beginning to tell her something about Joe, and her interrupting him, thrilled with her own news and wanting to share it. To impress him with her own success.

Well, I've really impressed him today, she thought bitterly. She could only imagine what the repercussions might be.

He handed over the draft of the new novel from his briefcase, and Penny received it as if it were holy writ, promising to read it and let him have an opinion in the next two weeks.

At last she looked across the table at Kate and smiled, apologetically. 'Sorry to be talking shop all the time.'

Kate shook her head. 'Don't be. It was my own fault for butting in like this,' she added haltingly, burningly aware of Ryan's ironic gaze.

GET A FREE TEDDY BEAR...

You'll love this plush, cuddly Teddy Bear, an adorable accessory for your dressing table, bookcase or desk. Measuring 5 ½" tall, he's soft and brown and has a bright red ribbon around his neck – he's completely captivating! And he's yours *absolutely free*, when you accept this no-risk offer!

▼ CLAIM YOUR FREE BOOKS AND FREE GIFT! RETURN THIS CARD TODAY! ▼

AND TWO FREE BOOKS!

Here's a chance to get **two free Harlequin Presents® novels** from the Harlequin Reader Service® absolutely free!

There's no catch. You're under no obligation to buy anything. We charge nothing – ZERO – for your first shipment. And you don't have to make any minimum number of purchases – not even one!

Find out for yourself why thousands of readers enjoy receiving books by mail from the Harlequin Reader Service®. They like the **convenience of home delivery**...they like getting the best new novels months before they're available in bookstores...and they love our **discount prices!**

Try us and see! Return this card promptly. We'll send your free books and a free Teddy Bear, under the terms explained on the back. We hope you'll want to remain with the reader service – but the choice is always yours!

306 HDL CTJ7

106 HDL CTJV
(H-P-10/99)

Name:		
	(PLEASE PRINT)	
Address:		Apt.#:
City:	State/Prov.:	Postal Zip/Code:

NO OBLIGATION TO BUY!

The Harlequin Reader Service® — Here's how it works:

Accepting your 2 free books and gift places you under no obligation to buy anything. You may keep the books and gift and return the shipping statement marked "cancel." If you do not cancel, about a month later we'll send you 6 additional novels and bill you just $3.12 each in the U.S., or $3.49 each in Canada, plus 25¢ delivery per book and applicable taxes if any.* That's the complete price and — compared to the cover price of $3.75 in the U.S. and $4.25 in Canada — it's quite a bargain! You may cancel at any time, but if you choose to continue, every month we'll send you 6 more books, which you may either purchase at the discount price or return to us and cancel your subscription.

*Terms and prices subject to change without notice. Sales tax applicable in N.Y. Canadian residents will be charged applicable provincial taxes and GST.

'Oh, no, I think it's good when a partner can be involved in a writer's career, at least at some level,' Penny said seriously. 'When he's absorbed in a book, you must feel very isolated.'

'Kate hasn't time to feel isolated.' Ryan leaned across to refill her glass before she had time to answer. 'She has her own career to occupy her.

'Oh?' Penny looked at her enquiringly. 'What is it that you do?'

'I'm a partner in a firm called Special Occasions,' Kate said quietly. 'Basically we organise parties and celebrations for people.'

'That must be terrific,' Penny laughed. 'Making people happy. Seeing them at their best.'

'It doesn't always happen.' Kate thought of the cancelled wedding. She glanced at her watch. 'And it's high time I got back to the office and did some more organising.'

She pushed back her chair and rose. 'But please don't let me break up the party. I'm sure you have a lot more to discuss.' She shared a taut smile between them both, and left.

Her intention was to get a taxi, but she still felt vaguely nauseous, so she decided to seek out the powder room first.

At any other time she'd have revelled in its unashamed opulence. Would have tested the comfort of the raspberry velvet sofa, and tried out the latest fragrances displayed in cut-glass flagons.

But all she wanted to do was rest her head against

the coolly tiled wall of her cubicle, and wait for the dizziness and churning to pass.

It seemed an eternity before she began to feel better. She emerged from the cubicle, went over to the vanity unit, and ran cold water into one of the basins, splashing it over her wrists and on to her face.

'Are you all right?'

With a start, Kate realised she'd been joined by Penny Barnes.

'Fine,' she returned ultra-brightly. 'I was just reviewing the amenities. Aren't they something? Over the top, or what?'

Penny laughed, but her expression was still concerned.

'You look awfully pale. Would you like me to get Ryan for you?'

'Heavens, no,' Kate said hastily. 'I promise you, I'm all right.'

'Well, I hope so. I wouldn't want to drag Ryan off to the north of England if you were going to be ill. It was good of him to step in at the last moment anyway.'

'Is that what he did?' Kate kept her tone casual, as she brushed a dusting of blusher across her cheekbones. 'He didn't mention it.' *Or the fact that he was going at all.*

Penny sighed. 'Yes, he's guest of honour at a thriller writers' convention in Yorkshire. It was supposed to be Louis Houghton, only he fell down some steps at his villa in the south of France last week, and busted his leg. Trying to emulate one of his heroes, according to his wife,' she added, rolling her eyes expressively. 'And Ryan, bless him, agreed to fill the breach.'

'Ah,' Kate said lightly. 'So that's how it all came about.'

'It's a pity you can't go with him. It's a lovely place, apparently, right on the edge of the Dales. But he said you wouldn't be able to get away.'

'It is rather short notice,' Kate agreed levelly. She summoned a smile of sorts. 'Well—goodbye, Miss Barnes. It was—good to meet you.' She took a deep breath. 'I'm sorry about the—the misunderstanding when I arrived.'

'Let's forget the whole thing.' The other's eyes were warm. 'And, to be accurate, it's Mrs Barnes, but I'd prefer Penny.'

'And please call me Kate.' She gave another constrained smile, and left.

Ryan was talking to the head waiter—probably being told what a vandal she was—and didn't notice her stealthy departure. She was lucky enough to pick up a cruising cab right outside the door, and directed the driver to take her to the boutique to pick up her other clothes as she sank thankfully into her seat.

Penny Barnes had been very nice about it all, she thought wretchedly. But then Ryan was an important author to Chatsworth Blair. Maybe she'd felt they had to humour her for his sake.

All the same, she wondered if Penny would share

the joke when she got back to her own office. 'My God, you should have seen her. Ryan should have put her into his next novel. The jealous wife. The bitch from hell.'

She shuddered. She'd been taught a lasting lesson today. Yet when she'd seen them together she'd been so sure. Thought she'd been so clever, tracing them to the restaurant...

The cab braked sharply to avoid a motorcycle courier, and Kate caught at the grab handle to steady herself, but thoughts jolted into place as well.

Because nothing had actually changed, she told herself sharply. Penny Barnes might not be Ryan's significant other, but someone else was. She had the evidence of the anonymous letter and the phone call she'd overhead to vouch for that.

This particular trail had been false, but some day soon she would pick up the right one, and the search would begin all over again.

Only, she thought, suddenly forlorn, I don't want it to.

And, closing her eyes, she felt the anguished prick of tears against her lids.

CHAPTER SIX

KATE was frankly dreading her return home that evening. Ryan was bound to be good and angry, and although she knew her suspicions were perfectly justified under the circumstances she could hardly tell him so.

Because he could simply deny any accusations she chose to fling at him. Or, he could admit everything, and leave her. Go to his other woman. And that was the last thing she needed to happen.

I want my marriage back, she thought fiercely. I'm not going to let it slip away because of one stupid lapse on Ryan's part. If that's all it is, of course, she amended, wincing. For all I know it could be the grand passion of his life.

But she couldn't let herself think in those terms. It hurt too much.

'Have a nice lunch? Is it somewhere we can use?' Louie asked brightly, coming in to collect a file.

Kate concealed a shudder. 'The food was good, but I didn't think it was big on atmosphere,' she returned rather wanly.

Louie played an elaborate game with some paperclips. 'Talking of food, as neither of us are working on Saturday, I wondered if you and Ryan would like

101

to come to dinner? It—it's a farewell banquet for Neil.'

Kate looked at her, startled. Neil had been a regular item in Louie's life for the past three months. 'Farewell?'

'He's taken a two-year contract in Saudi Arabia. It's quite understandable. He much prefers working in the field to pushing a pen at head office.'

Kate bit her lip. 'But don't you—mind?'

Louie shrugged. 'If only I did,' she responded candidly. 'It wasn't until he told me he was going that I realised how little involved we really were. Secondbest was probably as good as it was ever going to get.'

'Are you sure about that?' Kate asked wistfully.

Louie nodded. 'Certain,' she said levelly. 'Neil was still fixated on his previous girlfriend.'

'Oh, Lou, I'm sorry.'

'Don't be.' Lou sounded brisk. 'I was just as bad—hankering after someone I couldn't have either. We were both using each other as smokescreens to hide what we really wanted.'

Kate stared at her. 'I didn't know that,' she said slowly.

'It isn't something I was keen to spread about,' Louie said wryly. 'But I've realised life is too short to put on hold while someone decides whether or not his marriage is going to work. I don't have to settle for that.'

Kate winced. 'Of course you don't,' she said quietly. 'And I'm sure Saturday evening will be fine. I'd better check with Ryan, and call you this evening to confirm.'

That is, she reminded herself flatly, if Ryan ever speaks to me again.

When she let herself into the apartment, he was sitting facing the open windows, reading, a glass of wine on a table beside him.

From the kitchen came a tantalising aroma of tomatoes, garlic and herbs, and in spite of her jangled nerves, and uncertain stomach, Kate's nose twitched appreciatively.

Striving for normality—until the storm burst, anyway—she said, 'Something smells good.'

'I've made some meatballs to go with the pasta.' His tone was calm, even friendly. His face gave nothing away. But then it never had. Kate could remember a former colleague who'd worked with him in the City talking about Ryan's poker-face. 'It's what makes him such a great gambler,' he'd said.

But this time he was gambling with their marriage—their future together.

'I thought you could do with some solid food,' he added dryly. 'You didn't eat a great deal at lunch.'

She bit her lip. She'd thought he'd been too engrossed in his discussion with Penny Barnes to notice.

She said tautly, 'Well, that's hardly a surprise, is it?' She put down her bag and briefcase and came to stand directly in front of him. Her heart felt like a stone. 'Ryan—you've obviously got something to say.

Why don't you just get it over with? I'm a big girl. I can take it.'

There was a pause, then he said, 'I liked the dress.'

'So did I,' she said. 'And I hope its next owner will be just as pleased. I gave it to a charity shop.'

His brows lifted. 'A little drastic, isn't it?'

She shook her head. 'I'd never have worn it again. I hardly want a reminder of my less than finest hour.'

'I suppose not.' He paused again. 'As a matter of interest, why did you come in with all guns blazing?'

She swallowed. 'I—I was expecting to find you with Joe. Seeing you with—Penny threw me completely.'

'You don't usually overreact like that.' His eyes were cool and watchful. 'It was—spectacular.'

'Don't you laugh at me,' she said fiercely. 'Don't you dare bloody laugh, damn you.'

'Don't fool yourself, lady,' he bit back. He got to his feet in one lithe movement, and stood, hands on hips. 'I'm a long way from amusement, I promise you.'

The change was so sudden it rocked her, and she took a quick step backwards. He saw the reaction, and let his hands drop to his sides, his mouth twisting ruefully.

He said, 'Is there anything I could say that you haven't told yourself already?'

Kate bit her lip. 'I—shouldn't think so. And I'm truly sorry. I hope I haven't rocked any boats.'

'I think my sales figures can probably absorb the

shock waves.' He spoke lightly, but she wasn't fooled. 'Now, sit down, relax and have a glass of wine. Dinner will be about twenty minutes.'

She accepted the glass he handed to her with a small, tight smile then sat down on the sofa opposite, smoothing her skirt decorously over her knees.

'One thing intrigues me,' Ryan commented, refilling his own glass. 'How did you know where to find us?'

Kate groaned inwardly. Then, 'Elementary, my dear Watson,' she returned with an insouciance she was far from feeling. 'Remember that Hitchcock film festival we went to? When Cary Grant wanted to follow Eva Marie Saint in *North by Northwest*?'

'I do indeed,' Ryan said slowly. 'Well, well.' He lifted his glass to her in a mocking toast. 'If ever Special Occasions begins to pall, you could always take up private detection.'

Kate swallowed some wine. 'I don't think I'd be very good at it,' she returned. 'Too prone to jump to the wrong conclusions.'

'But why go to all that trouble? Even if I'd been meeting Joe instead of Penny, it was still just a business lunch. You don't usually bother.'

Now, if ever, was the moment to tell him about the anonymous letter. About all her doubts and fears ever since. About the even bleaker fear that their marriage was slipping away somehow. That the distance between them, widening every day, might soon be impossible to bridge.

Instead, she said, 'But I'm interested in your work. I always have been. I—I read the first one while you were writing it—remember?'

He smiled slowly, his gaze touching her with sudden frankly sensual reminiscence, making her skin tingle, and the breath catch softly in her throat.

'Yes,' he said. 'I remember.'

Ryan working at the table, she thought. Herself stretched out behind him on the old chaise longue, with its rubbed velvet and dented mahogany, that they'd bought for a song at auction and instantly dubbed the Casting Couch. Her eyes avidly scanning every page as it came from the printer.

Waiting for the moment when he would switch off the computer, and turn to her. 'What do you think?'

'I think it's brilliant, and you're wonderful.' She had no real idea whether it was or not. She could only hope. Tell him what he needed to hear, her arms reaching out to him, drawing him down to her in love and laughter, feeling the adrenalin that charged him, and reacting to it with eager passion. Her hands teasing, subtle as their bodies entwined...

'But you've read none of the others since.' The flat statement brought her hurtling back to the here and now. 'At least not in manuscript.'

'Well—there's been no need,' she said lamely. 'After all, you were an instant bestseller. An enormous success. And then you had Quentin—and Joe to discuss your work with. People who knew what they were talking about.'

He said softly, 'But they couldn't match your individual input, Katie.' He paused, then added with a certain deliberation, 'I'm amazed the old couch survived.'

To her own amazement, she realised she was blushing, her whole body suddenly charged by the memories he was evoking.

She said hurriedly, 'And of course I had my own career to think about too. And then we moved here.' Her laugh sounded almost nervous. 'Everything— changed.'

There was a silence, then Ryan said quietly, 'I guess it did.' He put down his glass. 'I'll check on dinner.'

'Well?' There was a faint smile in Ryan's eyes as Kate put down her knife and fork with a sigh of repletion.

'Better than that,' she said. 'It was a terrific meal, Ryan. Thank you.'

'My pleasure. Just fresh fruit for dessert, I'm afraid.' He pushed a platter of nectarines, apricots and grapes towards her.

'I don't know whether I can.' Kate selected a nectarine and began to cut it into quarters, then paused. 'I nearly forgot. Louie wants us to go to dinner on Saturday. It seems Neil's going abroad to work, and this is a goodbye bash.'

There was a pause. Then, 'Is she very upset?' Ryan

leaned back in his chair, his fingers playing with the stem of his glass. 'Was he the man of her dreams?'

'Apparently not.' Kate bit her lip. 'It seems that all this time she's been secretly in love with a married man—and I never guessed.' She shook her head. 'I can hardly believe it. I thought I knew her better than anybody.'

'How much do any of us really know about each other?' There was an odd note in his voice. 'Did she tell you who it was?'

'No. That stays a secret. I got the feeling that he's been stringing her along. Letting her think he might leave his wife.' She sighed. 'Poor Louie.'

'Well, perhaps he will.' Ryan drew the fruit bowl towards him and took a bunch of grapes. 'Maybe he's just waiting for the right moment—if there is such a thing.'

Kate stared at him. 'Are you serious? You think he should walk out on his marriage?'

He shrugged. 'It sounds as if he's done that already. Having an affair is a kind of desertion.'

Her throat tightened. 'Yes—but if it was just a passing fling the marriage might survive.'

'I wonder if that's possible.' Ryan sounded meditative.

'I'm sure it is.' Kate spoke passionately. 'With goodwill on both sides.'

His brows lifted mockingly. 'Why, darling, are you defending this errant husband?'

'By no means,' she said, huskily. 'I'm on the side of the wife.'

'Without knowing the circumstances?' He tutted. 'She might be equally to blame if the relationship isn't working.'

'Or she might simply be living in a fool's paradise, without a clue what's going on,' Kate snapped.

'I thought your sympathy was actually with Louie,' he said mildly.

'Well, so it is,' she said hurriedly. 'I just wish she could meet the right man, and—and settle down.'

'Are you sure that's what you want?' His tone was dispassionate.

She put down the dissected nectarine and wiped her fingers on her napkin, staring at him. 'What on earth do you mean?'

He shrugged. 'I was thinking of your earlier comment—about everything changing. Perhaps the consequences might not altogether please you.'

'Nonsense,' Kate said roundly. 'I want Louie to be happy, that's all. Where's the harm in that?'

Ryan helped himself to another handful of grapes, his expression enigmatic. 'No harm at all. Anyway, we'll go round on Saturday and wave Neil off into oblivion. Let's lose no time about it.'

Kate hesitated. 'I understand that there isn't much to lose—before you go off to Yorkshire.'

His brows lifted appreciatively. 'The girl detective strikes again. Although I was planning to tell you this evening, anyway.'

'Tell me,' she said slowly. 'Not—ask me. Ask if I minded.'

Ryan shrugged. 'You lead such a busy life, darling. I didn't think you'd even notice my absence.' He paused. 'Besides, a short time apart could even be therapeutic. Give us both some space—some thinking time.'

Kate felt as if she'd been touched by an icy hand. 'Is that what you want?'

'I think it's what we both need.' His face was closed. She could not read his expression, or guess his ultimate intentions.

Why do you want space? she cried out silently. When we're already a thousand miles apart? And what do you need time to consider?

She wanted to ask if he was going alone, but her courage failed her.

Instead: 'Was this why you cooked the meal?' she enquired with forced lightness. 'To keep me sweet when the blow fell?'

Ryan shrugged again. 'Perhaps I'm just worried about your sudden loss of appetite,' he countered.

'A hangover from lunchtime,' she said. 'It's difficult to eat with one's foot wedged firmly in one's mouth.' She paused. 'Ryan—you won't say anything to Louie, will you? I mean about her lover. I don't think she meant to tell me.'

'I won't say a word,' he said lightly. 'Now sit down, and I'll bring you some coffee.'

'Such service.' She flashed him a smile. 'Maybe you should go away more often.'

His own grin was oblique. 'Maybe I will.'

He turned and went into the kitchen. Kate watched him go, aware that her heart was thudding, and that the ground seemed suddenly to be sliding away from under her feet.

Had he just issued a warning? she wondered. Was he telling her their marriage, too, was virtually finished? That his own life held a secret love, too? A love he could no longer resist?

She took a deep, steadying breath. Whatever Ryan might or might not mean, it seemed that, for the immediate future, he intended life to go on as usual.

And that's what I must do, she thought. Take things one day at a time. However impossible that is.

She got to her feet, and went to the phone.

'Louie?' she said lightly. 'We'll be delighted to have dinner on Saturday. Looking forward to it.'

Kate drew the brush through her hair, and allowed the shining strands to curve gently forwards around her face.

She had taken great care with her appearance for tonight's dinner party. As she'd had a free day, she'd booked herself in at a beauty salon for a top-to-toe pampering, including a body massage with aromatherapy oil.

The ideal thing for stress, she told herself. And it was undoubtedly tension which had caused the continuing bouts of nausea which had gone on plaguing her this week. Well, they couldn't be allowed to go on any more. She needed to be on top form, physically and mentally, if she was to convince Ryan that their marriage was worth saving.

After her gaffe over Penny Barnes, she'd made a valiant attempt to convince herself that her suspicions and fears were totally unfounded, and that the anonymous letter had been a piece of casual spite from some sad person with no life of their own.

And, on the surface, things appeared normal. She and Ryan shared a roof and, edgily, a bed, met briefly at breakfast and talked about their respective days over the evening meal which Kate made a point of being there to prepare.

But, while Ryan had been unswervingly kind and concerned during her recurring bouts of nausea, she was uneasily aware just the same that there was no real intimacy between them. That he seemed as far away as ever in other respects. Their conversation touched no depths and even the laughter rang hollow.

Once we walked towards each other, she thought. Now we seem to be constantly tiptoeing round, avoiding no-go areas.

Was this what happened in all marriages? she wondered painfully. Did everybody wake one morning and find that the burning impetus which had once sent them into each other's arms had cooled into a pale memory?

Not that she was sure she'd have been able to respond whole-heartedly even if he had reached for her, she realised, grimacing. Having to interrupt your love-making in order to dash off and be sick was about the unsexiest scenario possible.

But neither did she want to reach a stage where sharing a bed with him was simply a habit. If that happened, then the gulf between them was probably unbridgeable.

But I don't feel like that, she argued. I still want him so much, yet I'm scared to make the first move in case he turns me down again.

With hindsight, she bitterly regretted the destruction of the letter. Far better to have shown it to him, and risked the agony of his guilt, than attempt to live with this continuing uncertainty.

At least, she thought, I would have known...

And Ryan was busy, of course, she reminded herself, preparing the notes for his seminar, as well as making the slight changes to his latest script that Penny had suggested.

Both Quentin and Penny were full of enthusiasm for the book, predicting it would be his top seller yet, and the contract that was being drawn up reflected this.

Kate had been embarrassed to find the time and place of each meeting with agent and publisher elaborately circled in red on the phone pad.

Altogether, it had been a strange week, with a sudden influx of enquiries at work—enough to fill their schedule to the end of the year and beyond.

Once she'd have been thrilled. Now, for the first time, the success of the company wasn't her major priority.

Louie seemed preoccupied too. Maybe the prospect of Neil's departure had affected her more deeply than she'd bargained for, Kate mused without particular conviction. Or perhaps she was considering ways and means of winning over the man she really loved.

She stood up, viewing herself critically in the mirror. The dress she'd chosen wasn't new, but it was one that Ryan had always liked, unashamedly sexy in soft black crêpe, with a deep neckline, and a wrap-around skirt which fastened on one hip with its own sash.

Her stockings were black too, as was the sinuous new lingerie she'd treated herself to.

She'd shadowed her eyes and applied blusher with meticulous care, and her mouth glowed like some scented, mysterious rose.

And if this doesn't work I'll give up, she thought as she turned away to pick up her bag.

Except that she wouldn't do any such thing. She would fight and go on fighting to keep Ryan with every breath in her body until all hope was gone. And beyond.

She felt ridiculously self-conscious as she went downstairs.

Ryan was on the phone, talking to the organiser of the seminar. 'I should be with you around lunchtime,' he was saying. 'We can go over the final details then. Cheers.'

He replaced the receiver, and turned. As he caught sight of her, she saw his eyes widen—become suddenly intent. Felt the air between them shiver with awareness, and something more.

Her breasts strained against the silk which confined them. A deep quiver of need ran down her body to her loins.

Her voice shook slightly. 'How do I look?'

The last time she'd worn this dress, she'd asked the same question, spinning round on one high-heeled foot, her eyes, her voice, her entire body language teasing and provocative.

'Do I look good?' she'd prompted, with all the confidence of sexual power.

'Good enough to eat,' he'd told her huskily. He'd crossed the room to her, his hands loosening the sash of the dress and sliding beneath it to find the warm, moist core of her, while his mouth took leisurely toll of hers. He'd kissed her throat, pushing away the deep V of her neckline with his lips so that he could explore her breasts.

They'd been due at a book-launch party for another of Quentin's authors, and they'd been hideously late. Her whole being bloomed with the memory of it.

Remember too, she cried out to him, silently, pleadingly. Remember how it always was between us. How it can be again.

He said slowly, 'You look—breathtaking.' His eyes

touched her, lingering on the shape of her breasts, the subtle lines of her thighs beneath the clinging crêpe. Then he turned his glance, instead, on his watch. 'And the cab I ordered should be downstairs.'

'We could always send it away.' She felt the pulse leap in her throat, as she fought to regain his attention. To fuel the desire she'd sensed in the sudden heat of his regard. To build on this moment.

His brows lifted. 'We could,' he agreed. 'But that wouldn't be very polite to Louie, who's expecting us, and who seems to need all the consideration we can muster right now.'

She'd already swallowed her pride. Now, disappointment left an equally bitter taste.

Her voice sounded brittle. 'You're right, of course. We'd better go. We don't want to be late.'

She picked up her jacket and bag, and walked, head held high, to the door.

Trying to ignore the voice in her head, which whispered that it might already be too late—for both of them.

CHAPTER SEVEN

IT PROBABLY wasn't the worst dinner party she'd ever attended, Kate reflected afterwards. But if not it ran a close second.

Louie had welcomed them extravagantly, her generous curves swathed in pillarbox-red, which she'd accessorised with a determined smile that seemed to have been nailed there.

Maybe she'd suddenly discovered she was going to miss Neil more than she thought, Kate had thought ruefully, pinning on her own delighted expression.

The food had been delicious as always, with chilled avocado soup preceding seafood served with pasta in a thick, creamy sauce, enriched with cheese, and a fresh fruit salad to follow.

Kate had made herself eat and praise, as if she didn't have a care in the world beyond the next mouthful, wanting the almost hectic cheerfulness of her voice to drown out the fierce drumming of her own heartbeat. The frightened questions spiralling in her mind.

Across the table, she'd watched Ryan covertly, endlessly from under her lashes, trying to see beyond the cool mask, but failing. Searching for answers she could not find.

But then he'd barely offered an unprompted word for the duration of the meal.

Perhaps his silence indicated that he too realised they had reached some kind of watershed in their relationship, Kate thought, agony twisting inside her.

And all the time, somehow, she'd gone on chatting and laughing. Asking Neil about his new job. Teasing him about the exacting Saudi alcohol laws. Exclaiming over the leisure facilities and fringe benefits at the complex where he'd be based.

She'd be lucky if she had any voice left tomorrow.

Yet, in spite of her efforts, the atmosphere round the table had borne all the hallmarks of a wake.

Neil, too, had been much quieter than usual, his responses muted. Even his enthusiasm for this new departure had seemed wan.

Yes, he'd agreed, it was all a step into the unknown.

'But against that you have to weigh the value of what you're leaving behind,' he added. 'And I realised it was no contest.'

There was a brief awkward silence, broken eventually by Louie collecting the plates together.

It was almost a relief when, after coffee, he excused himself on the grounds he still had packing to do.

'Not one of my better ideas,' said Louie, as Kate helped her load the dishwasher.

'Are you sure you want him to go?' Kate asked carefully.

Louie sighed. 'I've no strong feelings either way. I

realised months ago that Neil was like one of those dresses you keep hanging in the back of the wardrobe, because it might look good if you lost a stone in weight and changed your hair colour.'

Kate winced. 'He seems to have regrets.'

'I think he signed the contract as a grand gesture to Helen, his ex.' Louie pulled a face. 'Hoping that the threat of his departure would bring her running back with tears of remorse. Trouble is—she's moved on, and so should he. He's a genuinely nice guy, and will make some woman a smashing husband.'

'But not you.'

Louie shook her head. 'Never in this world.'

Kate paused. 'Are you still thinking about this other man?' she asked gently.

Louie nodded jerkily, her eyes fixed on the floor. 'I keep wondering if I should have tried harder. Actually made him choose. Then at least I'd have known...'

'Is it too late to find out?'

'I don't know.' Louie kept her gaze averted. 'Maybe I'm scared of rocking the boat. Of coping with the consequences.'

'But if his marriage isn't working... If he's not happy, his wife wouldn't want to keep him tied to her, surely.'

Louie's mouth twisted. 'Wouldn't she? Who's to say she's noticed that anything's wrong? She may have put down any cracks in the relationship to normal wear and tear. And maybe that's all it ever was anyway.'

Kate hesitated. 'Are there any children involved?'

'No.' Louie shook her head. 'I think that may have been a major part of the problem. He wanted a family. She preferred a career.'

Kate bit her lip. 'Of course, you haven't heard her side of it.'

'As I've told myself repeatedly. Not that it helps, particularly.'

'So what are you going to do?'

Louie sighed harshly. 'Right now I'm going to clear the rest of the table, while you make us some more extra-strong coffee.'

'But you're obviously going to think about it.' Kate put a comforting hand on Louie's rigid shoulder.

'Yes,' Louie said quietly. 'I think I have to—whatever the cost.' She raised miserable eyes and looked at Kate. 'Do you think I'm wrong?'

'I don't feel I can make any moral judgement about this,' Kate said gently. 'I—I don't know what I'd do in your place. But, whatever you decide, I'll be on your side.'

Louie gave her a taut little grimace of a smile and went out of the room.

Left to herself, Kate filled the coffee machine, and switched it on. Her spirits were heavy as she rinsed the cups they'd been using, then placed them on a tray. It worried her that she hadn't been aware of

Louie's problems at the time. Hadn't realised what the other woman had clearly been suffering.

God, but I've become self-centred, she castigated herself.

And she couldn't make the excuse that she had troubles of her own because this affair had clearly taken place long before her life had started to come apart at the seams.

She opened the fridge and studied the sparse contents. Louie was an impulse cook, buying ingredients fresh, and using them instantly. She wasn't a store cupboard person, as the fridge testified. There were a few eggs, some yoghurt, milk and the remains of the carton of cream they'd used in their coffee. And, of course, three bottles of champagne—the only other staple she was never without, Kate thought affectionately as she extracted the cream.

She refilled the jug, then carried the tray through to the living room. As she shouldered her way into the room, she saw Louie and Ryan standing together by the window, close but not touching.

He was talking to her softly and urgently as she stared up at him, her face suddenly naked and vulnerable in a way Kate had never seen before.

Both of them, she realised, too absorbed to even be aware of her motionless presence in the doorway.

She wanted to say, Hi—remember me? Something cheerful and normal that would cut the tension that filled the room. That would turn their attention—her husband—her friend—back to her. But no words would come.

The scent of the coffee drifted up to her, and she knew that she would never be able to smell coffee again without remembering this moment. But without quite knowing why.

She made herself walk forward and put the tray on the table, and the chink of the crockery brought Ryan's head sharply round.

'Fresh supplies,' she announced with deliberate cheerfulness. 'Come and get it.'

'You were quick.' Louie was smiling but there were bright flags of colour flying in her cheeks, a sure sign of inner disturbance. As if she and Ryan had been having a row about something...

They sat round the table, as they'd done so many times, to dissect the evening that had just passed, but somehow it was different this time. The laughter seemed to ring hollow, and there were too many silences.

Only the tension stayed the same. Kate felt it grate like emery against her senses.

For a moment, the breath caught in her throat, then she launched herself gamely into speech, enthusing hectically about all the work which had come flooding in lately, describing some of the clients, along with their foibles, and their more unrealistic demands. Making them sound fun as well as funny.

'And the really great thing is that many of them have come on recommendation,' Kate added, with a smile that made her lips ache. 'Our fame must be spreading. At this rate we'll soon be taking bookings into the millennium.'

Ryan stirred some cream into his coffee. 'My congratulations.' His tone was meditative. 'You've achieved the goal of the Nineties. You're now a completely independent woman.'

She stared at him, aware that his mouth was set almost grimly. 'You—you make it sound like a life sentence.'

'I'm not sure it isn't,' Louie said unexpectedly.

Kate tried to laugh, and failed. 'You're joking, surely. We're a success. Going from strength to strength.'

'In order to achieve what?'

Kate hesitated. 'Well—our place in the market. Financial security.'

'Oh, really?' Louie sounded bitter. 'I just hope we think it's worth it.' She caught Kate's incredulous glance and shrugged defensively. 'I'm sorry, love. That doesn't apply to you. You have an alternative.'

'I do?' Kate was floundering.

'I think she means me,' Ryan said very gently. 'Our marriage.'

'Oh.' Kate felt suddenly numb. 'Oh, yes, of course.'

'Of course,' Ryan echoed softly and mockingly. 'And on that note, my sweet, shall we return to the marital home, and let Louie get some rest?'

*   *   *

From her corner of the taxi, Kate said uncertainly, 'Did you and Louie have a fight?'

'What makes you think that?' The dark figure in the opposite corner was very still.

'Things just seemed—awkward back there.' An understatement if ever there was one.

He was silent for a moment. 'Perhaps it was just that kind of evening.'

She said, 'So, are you going to tell me about it?'

'I think you already know.' His tone was dry.

'You mean, she was telling you about her other man?' Kate couldn't keep the surprise out of her voice. 'What she's planning to do?'

'That came into it.'

'But why should she talk to you about it?'

'Why not? You did, after all.'

'But that's different,' Kate said lamely, after a pause. 'You're my husband. I tell you everything.'

'Do you, darling? How flattering.'

'And don't joke. This isn't funny.'

'I never thought it was.' There was a sudden harshness in his voice. 'I gather you've been advising her to follow her heart's desire, and to hell with the consequences.'

'Not exactly.'

'I'm relieved to hear it.'

She gasped. 'I like that. You were the one who said that if he'd been unfaithful the marriage was probably rocky anyway.'

'But I don't necessarily advocate Louie giving it an

extra shove either,' Ryan came back to her grittily. 'You shouldn't have interfered, Kate.'

'And how do you describe your own intervention?' she demanded bitterly. 'A spot of homespun brotherly advice?'

'Not far off,' he said tersely. 'I told her to be careful. To make very sure this was what she really wanted. Because the consequences could be catastrophic.'

'You have wisdom beyond your years.'

'What makes me think you don't mean that?' He paused. 'Not that it matters. Because the one who needs wisdom is Louie.'

'She'll do the right thing,' Kate said confidently.

'I hope you'll still think so in the days to come,' Ryan said shortly, and relapsed into silence.

Kate huddled into her corner, her mind engaged on the now familiar treadmill of disturbing thoughts. Ryan's shift of ground over Louie's confidences had surprised her, but in many ways it was the least of her worries.

She should be devoting all her attention to bridging the ever-increasing distance between them. She certainly couldn't afford to fall out with him over a problem that had no direct bearing on either of them.

They rode up in the lift without a word, but as Kate walked ahead of him into the apartment she said, 'Ryan, I—I don't want us to quarrel.'

'We can't always be in agreement, Katie.' His voice was gentle.

'But these days we always seem to be at odds.' She dropped her jacket on to a sofa, and wheeled to face him. 'You must feel that.'

'I certainly think a few days apart could be salutary.' Ryan discarded his own jacket, and loosened his tie.

'A few days,' she echoed bitterly. 'We've been apart for weeks already. Or haven't you noticed?'

He said quietly, 'Yes, I've noticed.'

'But you don't do anything about it.' Kate took a step towards him. 'There was a time when you'd have asked me to go to Yorkshire with you.'

'I thought you were snowed under with work. That's the message from this evening.' He gave her a level look. 'And you've never invited me to accompany you on any of your own weekends away.'

'That's rather different,' she protested. 'I'm always there in an official capacity.'

'Whereas I, of course, am travelling north for my health.' His tone was ironic.

She said wearily, 'I didn't mean that. I know you're the guest of honour—the visiting lecturer.' She tried to smile. 'I could bask in your reflected glory.'

He shook his head. 'Not this time, Katie.'

Her mouth was dry. Her heart seemed to be pulsing unevenly. But she lifted her chin in challenge. 'You really don't want me, do you?'

His brows lifted. 'Is that what you think? Because you couldn't be more wrong.' He came to her in two quick strides, his hands strong and urgent on her body as he pulled her towards him. 'All night, I've been watching you,' he muttered. 'Thinking about you, and what I'd do once we were alone.'

He kissed her heatedly, demandingly, his lips parting hers with the familiarity of possession, bending her backwards over his arm so that his lips could caress the long line of her throat, while one hand reached down to tug open the sash that fastened her dress.

As the yielding fabric fell apart, Ryan looked down at her, the breath rasping in his throat as he caught sight of the scraps of black silk that clothed her—the camisole cut starkly low over her breasts, the high-legged panties that barely concealed her sex, the lace-topped stockings.

'God.' The word was torn from him almost in anguish. 'Do you know—have you the least bloody idea how beautiful you are? How completely and utterly desirable?'

His hands took her hips, pulling her against his body, against the strength and force of his erection, as the unwanted dress fell to the floor.

His hand twisted in her hair as he brought her mouth to his again. His tongue sought hers, his teeth grazing the softness of her lower lip.

Kate was rocked—off-balance, emotionally as well as physically, as she responded to his kisses. After the days and nights of virtual estrangement, this sudden onslaught on her senses was almost too powerful. She felt overwhelmed—carried away on some uncontrollable tide of feeling—her whole body in tumult.

The breath caught in her throat as Ryan pushed away the narrow straps of the camisole to seek the offered enticement of her breasts, his hands cupping her, moulding the delicate flesh, making her nipples harden to aching delight under the play of his fingers.

His mouth was on the pulse below her ear, the curve of her shoulder. Her head fell back helplessly against his supporting arm as he began to caress her breasts with his lips, his tongue a subtle flame inciting the swollen peaks to new raptures.

His hand slid down over her stomach to find the dampened silk covering the sweet molten core of her. To explore with one questing fingertip the full scalding heat of her arousal.

Kate felt her body shudder in primeval response. She opened herself blindly to the exquisite pleasure of his caress, thrusting herself, gasping, against his hand.

Her hands moved on him in their turn, dragging his clothing apart. A button ripped from his shirt, and went spinning to the floor. She was clumsy with his zip, but at last she succeeded, fingers closing round him, stroking him, every movement a silent, almost desperate importunity for the ultimate fulfilment that she craved.

When he began to lower her to the rug, she sank beneath him, boneless, mindless. Oblivious to everything but the sensations he was engendering. To her own delirious reply.

He peeled away the scraps of black silk, leaving her naked except for the stockings, which formed an erotic contrast to her creamy flesh. And she helped him shed his own clothes, eager to feel his hair-roughened skin against her own.

The musky masculine fragrance of him filled her nose and mouth. So familiar and, at the same time, so mysterious. So infinitely precious.

Kate laid her mouth against his shoulder, tasting his skin. Her fingertips caressed his back, tracing the line of fine hair which marked his spine, relishing the strength of bone and play of muscle. Feathering her hands over the flat male buttocks, and the long hard flanks.

Ryan was kissing her body, marking a lazy trail between her breasts, down to the hollow of her navel. And further, making her body arch in voluptuous delight as his tongue teased and lured her.

'Ryan.' Her voice sounded small—strangled—as she pulled his head away from her. She was so near, and she wanted him inside her in the usual pattern of their lovemaking—joining her on the path to their mutual pleasure.

'Wait.' He smiled at her, and lowered his head again. She felt the warmth of his breath against the delicate skin of her inner thigh. 'Give yourself.' His voice was low, husky. 'Come for me.'

She wanted to protest, but it was too late. All the

wicked, beautiful things he was doing to her were coalescing into one ecstatic spiral of feeling. She gave a cry of sheer abandonment as her whole being shuddered to the deep pulsation of her climax.

When the world steadied itself, there were tears on her face, and he dried them with the sleeve of his torn shirt. Kate tried to say something, but he laid a silencing finger on her parted lips.

He began to kiss her again, very gently, just brushing her forehead, her eyelids, her cheekbones and her lips with his mouth, while his hand stroked her throat, her breasts, the curve of her elbow, and the back of her knee.

And deep within she sensed the first stirrings of renewed excitement.

She whispered, 'Shall we go to bed?'

'Later.'

'It—it's too soon for me.'

'It won't be.'

His caresses were becoming more deliberately sensual. More adventurous. But when she tried to follow his lead, pleasure him in turn with her hands and lips, Ryan shook his head, capturing her wrists, and holding them above her head.

For a moment, startled, she considered resistance, but as his tantalising, deliciously prolonged exploration of her body continued it was, she realised breathlessly, much easier and infinitely more enjoyable to let him have his way. It was even becoming—necessary...

And not, she discovered with real shock, too soon at all.

Her whole body seemed to sigh with joy as he entered her. He moved inside her smoothly, fluidly, drawing her into his rhythm, then increasing it by subtle degrees, thrusting deeper and deeper still.

Her skin slicked with sweat, Kate wound her arms round his shoulders, locked her legs round his waist, holding him within her, driving herself and him to some passionate point of no return.

Every sense, every nerve-ending was focussed and intense. Their mouths were fierce, almost feral in their demand, each of the other. No quarter was being asked, or given.

This time, as their control fragmented, the spasms which convulsed her body seemed on the point of tearing her apart. She heard Ryan cry out, his voice breaking on her name.

They lay for a long time in each other's arms without speaking, her head pillowed on his chest, his lips against her hair.

'Are you cold?'

She'd only shivered slightly, but he'd noticed.

'A little bit.' She sat up, feeling oddly shy. 'And I feel silly wearing these stockings and nothing else. As if I was a centrefold in a magazine.'

Ryan grinned lazily. 'You look amazing. My own private fantasy.'

She reached for her dress, slid her arms into the

sleeves. 'We've never done this before. Made love down here, that is.'

'Then we should have done.' Ryan pushed aside her skirt to drop a last swift kiss on the pale skin above her stocking-top. 'At least this bloody rug's justified its existence at last.'

He got to his feet in one lithe movement, supremely unselfconscious about his own nakedness, and pulled her up to face him. 'Can you make it up the stairs, or do you want to be carried?'

'Have you got the strength?' Kate pantomimed surprise.

His answering smile was wolfish. 'Just try me.'

'I thought I already had.'

'The night's still young.'

'That,' she said, 'is a boast I might ask you to make good.'

'And the pleasure,' he said, 'will quite definitely *not* be all mine.'

He put his arm round her waist, and walked with her up to their bedroom. Kate's body was glowing with fulfilment, but, more importantly, deep within her was a tiny blossoming of something that could be hope—or even happiness.

She thought with new confidence, Everything will be all right now. It has to be...

CHAPTER EIGHT

KATE awoke slowly, stretching, boneless as a cat, as she dreamily absorbed the feeling of total well-being that suffused her.

Eyes closed against the intrusive sunlight filtering into the bedroom, she let her mind drift back over the events of the previous night, her mouth curving in gleeful reminiscence.

Making love with Ryan had always been good, but lately—maybe—it had become a little cosy and domestic. Just a bit *married*. But last night had changed all that—had opened up a whole new dimension, she admitted, burrowing deeper into the mattress with a small sensuous wriggle.

They might have been strangers meeting for the first time, searching out each other's most intimate secrets with eager, untiring hunger. Using their mutual pleasure to lift each other to undreamed-of heights.

At times, her capacity to incite as well as respond had almost frightened her. There had been a wildness in Ryan that was close to darkness, and some hidden, unguessed-at side of her had surged to meet him.

As her hand was reaching across the bed to encounter him now. Except...

Kate's eyes snapped open, and she sat up staring at the empty space in the bed beside her.

Except that Ryan wasn't there. And her disappointment was almost absurd.

She had a clear memory of his arms around her and his lips against her hair as she'd finally fallen asleep. Surely, this of all mornings, she had the right to expect to find him close to her when she woke. Especially considering the state of total exhaustion they'd both been reduced to, she remembered with a small delicious shiver. She'd have thought he would have slept until noon.

And—if he wasn't here—where was he?

For a moment, she was very still, listening for clues—unable to detect the reassurance of the shower running in the bathroom. She gave Ryan's rumpled pillow an uneasy look, wondering if she could have imagined the whole glorious, sensual experience.

Then she heard unmistakable sounds of movement from the floor below, and relaxed.

Of course, he was getting ready for his trip. After all, she'd heard him speaking to the organiser, arranging to be in Yorkshire by lunchtime. Naturally, he'd had to get up early, no matter what his energy level.

Her lips quirked as she threw back the covers. And she too would have to move with the speed of light if she was going with him. As she fully intended to do. She had holiday due, after all, and Louie could hold the fort for a few days. Maybe it would even help keep her mind off her problems.

Whatever, there's no way I'm letting Ryan out of my sight, she thought mischievously. Not any more.

She noticed, cheeks warming slightly, that she was still wearing those stockings.

Rather too decadent for the cold light of day, and laddered beyond redemption, she decided, slipping them off before she reached for her robe.

As she reached the foot of the stairs, she stood, looking about her, feeling oddly shy. Wanting Ryan to come to her—to hold her. To teach her by the caress of his mouth on hers that last night had been no dream, but heated, golden reality.

His leather travel bag was waiting, already strapped up, in the middle of the floor. And the door to his study was standing ajar.

Kate trod quietly over, and peeped in. Ryan was at his desk, putting files into his briefcase. As the door creaked slightly, he turned, brows raised, and looked at her.

'Did I disturb you? I'm sorry. I meant to let you have your sleep.'

His voice was brisk, almost impersonal, Kate thought, jolted. It was certainly not the greeting she'd anticipated.

She summoned a smile. Infused warmth, huskiness into her voice. 'Well, my plan was rather different.' She glanced at her watch. 'How long can you give me to warn Louie, and throw a few things in a bag?'

There was a pause as Ryan fastened his briefcase. He said evenly, 'Why should you want to do that?'

'Because I've decided to come with you—to your convention.' She laughed, pushing her hair back from her face. 'I don't know whether Yorkshire would have been my ideal choice for a second honeymoon, but I'll make the most of whatever's available.'

She paused, vainly searching his face for overt signs of delight. 'Is something wrong? Aren't your pleased I want to be with you?'

'I'm delighted.' His tone was dry. 'Unfortunately, it's not going to be possible.' He sent her a swift smile that barely curved his mouth. 'Another time, perhaps.'

It was a beautiful sunlit morning, but Kate found she was hugging her arms round her body for warmth.

She said slowly, 'If I didn't know better, I'd say I was getting the brush-off.'

'Not at all. We both have separate careers. Sometimes they take us in different directions.' Ryan shrugged. 'This is one of those times, that's all.'

'You seem,' she said, 'to be taking this very much in your stride.'

'It's certainly no big deal,' he retorted, slotting his laptop computer into its carrying case. 'You've already made it clear how busy you are at work. Can you afford to leave the goldmine untended? Anyway, you'd be bored to extinction,' he added dismissively. 'As well as the lectures and seminars, I've been asked to take a couple of workshop sessions for aspiring writers.' He slanted an edged smile at her. 'And we both know that you're not too keen on them.'

'Does it still rankle?' Kate drew a deep breath. 'The fact that I didn't want you to throw up your City job?'

'A little more faith would have been appreciated.'

'But I did believe in you,' she protested. 'I believed in your writing.'

'But not in my ability to succeed at it.' His voice was ironic. 'You'd have preferred it to remain a nice little hobby, quite outside the day job. Something to keep me at home in the evenings.'

She winced. 'I was frightened,' she said defensively. *And I still am now but it's about something completely different.* 'I've never pretended otherwise,' she went on quickly. 'It seemed such a risk.'

'I took them every day at the office.' His voice was harsh. 'Quite desperate risks. With the kind of money you can't even allow yourself to think about. But because you didn't know about them they didn't worry you.'

She said incredulously, 'And this—this is why you don't want me to go with you to Yorkshire?'

'No,' he said. 'I thought we agreed we both needed some space.'

'If that's the case,' Kate said, 'then, may I ask, what was last night all about?'

'I thought—sex,' he said. 'Satisfying a mutual need. Or is it a trick question?'

Was that what he thought? her stunned brain demanded. Could he really dismiss all that ravishment and delight—the giving and taking of passionate love—as the mere gratification of an appetite? Was that all that it had meant to him? All that she meant to him—something to be used—then discarded the following morning as an irrelevance?

Pain twisted like a knife inside her.

Her voice shook. 'You—you bastard. How dared you treat me like that? As if I was some kind of tart.'

'Because I thought you were on offer. The dress— the underwear seemed to be sending out unmistakable signals.' His mouth twisted cynically as he surveyed her. 'I hope I didn't misread them. God forbid I should do anything politically incorrect.'

She lifted her chin, glaring at him. 'Get out of here,' she said unsteadily. 'Go to bloody Yorkshire— and stay there. Take all the space you want. And I don't care if you never come back.'

'How fickle of you, darling,' Ryan drawled. 'Only a moment ago you were talking of second honeymoons.'

'That,' she said, 'was when I thought we might still have a marriage. Not a sick joke.'

She turned and went out of the room, and up the stairs, trying not to stumble on the hem of her robe. She reached the bed, and sat down on its edge, aware that her legs probably wouldn't support her any more.

Listening for the sound of Ryan following her. Coming to make his peace. Their peace. Wanting to bury her face in his shoulder and tell him that she didn't mean it.

To reach, mentally, the kind of attunement that they'd experienced physically the night before.

Or had she simply been fooling herself about that? she wondered wearily. Men, after all, viewed these things so differently. So basically. A need to be fulfilled, nothing more. Maybe she'd imagined the spiritual and emotional dimension involved.

Even so, she couldn't let him leave like this. Pride didn't matter. She would have to make the first conciliatory move. Call to him. Ask something neutral— like when the convention was due to end...

Anything—no matter how trivial—that would bring him to her side. That would give her a chance to make amends.

And to persuade him to take her with him. To convince him that they needed to talk. Communication, she thought, instead of the chill silence of separation.

She got slowly to her feet, tightening the sash of her robe, steeling herself.

And heard, as she did so, the quiet, inexorable sound of the flat door closing.

'Ryan.' Her voice sounded frantic, echoing back from the high roof space. She ran down the stairs, praying that it was a mistake. That he hadn't left, after all.

But the flat was empty, and Ryan was gone.

And for the first time, she realised numbly, she had no guarantee that he was ever coming back.

It was the longest day she'd ever spent in her life. She used up a lot of it just huddled in the corner of the sofa, staring dry-eyed into space, or wandering into the kitchen to make yet another cup of coffee which the tightness in her throat wouldn't allow her to swallow.

She'd heard the phrase 'being in limbo' many times, but now she was discovering what it meant.

She needed someone to talk to. Someone to tell her that everything would be all right. Instant reassurance.

She rang Louie, but only got her answering machine.

She even telephoned Ryan's mother. If she said she was alone, maybe Mrs Lassiter would ask her over there, she thought hopefully.

She wanted to sit in Ryan's old home, with his family round her. She needed to absorb some of the kind harmony of their life into her own troubled soul. But there was no reply.

Everyone had gone, it seemed. And only she was left.

She began to watch the time obsessively, calculating over and over again how long it would take Ryan to reach his destination. How soon it would be possible for him to pick up the phone and call her.

He'd said he would be there around lunchtime, from the snatch of conversation she'd overheard. So she'd have to allow him some extra time to settle into his room. To do all the usual social things. And then he'd call her—wouldn't he? Surely he wouldn't take her parting remarks to him at their face value.

Yes, she'd been hurt and disappointed, but her reaction had been way over the top. He'd know that, and make allowances, surely.

It was late afternoon before she was prepared to admit that her optimism was unfounded. That there probably wasn't going to be any phone call.

'Right,' Kate said through gritted teeth. 'Then the mountain will go to Mohammed.'

She'd seen all the literature about the convention, so she knew the name of the old country house in the Dales where he was staying. A simple call to Directory Enquiries gave her the number.

'Allengarth Centre,' said a woman's friendly voice. 'How can I help you?'

'I'd like to speak to Ryan Lassiter, please.'

There was a short pause, then the voice said, 'I'm sorry, but he hasn't arrived yet.'

'But you were expecting him at lunchtime, weren't you?' Kate's voice sharpened with anxiety.

The other laughed. 'Bless you, no. The convention starts with dinner tomorrow evening. Mr and Mrs Lassiter are due here for that. Not before.'

Kate's throat felt suddenly paralysed. She said huskily, 'I'm sorry. I—I didn't realise Mrs Lassiter was with him.'

'Oh, yes,' the woman said comfortably. 'He made that clear when he agreed to come. We have a very nice suite for our principal guests when they bring a partner.' She paused. 'May I pass on a message when they arrive?'

'No, thank you.' Kate steadied herself with a supreme effort. 'It can wait.'

It took several moments for her to replace the receiver on its rest. Her hands didn't seem to be coordinating with her brain.

No wonder he hadn't wanted her to go with him, she thought numbly. He had very different plans. Beginning with a leisurely journey north, staying in one of the intimate country pubs that he'd once enjoyed with her.

The Royal Oak at Stretton Hulme, she found herself remembering. That was Ryan's favourite. And they'd be there by now, strolling along the path by the river, watching the swans and the moorhens, before returning to the big first-floor room, with its four-poster bed, and the adjoining old-fashioned bathroom with its tub that had plenty of room for two...

She pressed her fist against her mouth, stifling the moan of pain that these images evoked.

Surely—oh, please, God—Ryan wouldn't have taken her there. Not to a place which had meant so much to them as a couple. Where they'd always vowed to return.

But then, what was one more betrayal amongst so many? she asked herself bitterly.

And last night had been the greatest—most searing betrayal of all.

How could he, in conscience, make love to her like that when he was planning to spend a few illicit days with his mistress—that significant other who had shadowed every day of her life for the past weeks?

Unless it was a farewell performance, of course. Something to remember him by.

And I sent him away, she thought with anguish. I practically gave him permission to leave.

She was walking backwards and forwards, her arms wrapped round her body in protection and support, her mind dazed—spinning.

And she had at least twenty-four endless hours to endure before she could even go up to Yorkshire and confront them. If that was what she was going to do...

Yet what other choice did she have? She'd been made a fool of long enough. Now it was time to fight back.

She couldn't bring herself to eat, but she needed something to dispel the inner chill, and restore her strength. Eventually, she heated up a pan of tinned tomato soup—the ultimate comfort food.

Nor could she bear to spend the night in their bed. Instead she found a spare quilt and pillow, and made herself a makeshift nest on the sofa, where a sleeping pill eased her into a restless, dream-laden sleep.

She awoke the next morning with a slight headache, and for a moment she was tempted to ring the office and tell them she would not be in. The thought of facing Louie and Debbie and having to pretend everything was all right made her stomach churn.

But the prospect of another day in the flat, pacing up and down, and tormenting herself with images of

Ryan and his other woman, was equally unbearable, so, eventually, she swallowed some paracetamol and, heavy-eyed, took a cab to work.

Debbie met her with a long face. 'Louie's not coming in,' she reported. 'There was a message on the machine when I arrived saying she isn't well.'

Tell me about it, Kate said silently, and was immediately smitten with self-reproach. After all, Louie had her problems too, she reminded herself sadly, and her sickness was probably of the heart.

Determined, she plunged into the pile of work waiting for her, using it both as a palliative and a shield against the darkness hovering always on the edge of her vision.

She waited until late afternoon, then phoned the Allengarth Centre again, and this time a man answered.

'Good afternoon.' She kept her voice level. 'May I speak to Mrs Lassiter please?'

Her heart was thumping raggedly as she waited to be connected.

Then, 'I'm sorry, madam.' The man's voice again. 'There's no answer from their suite.'

'But they are there?' Her free hand was gripping the edge of the desk so tightly that her knuckles stood out, stark and white.

'Mr Lassiter's name is in the register, madam. Will you try later? Or can I take a message?'

'No,' Kate said quietly. 'No message.'

She told Debbie she was leaving early, and went

round the corner to the florist. She had to talk to someone or burst, and Louie seemed the obvious candidate. While the assistant was wrapping her flowers, Kate popped next door to the off licence and bought some wine as well. They could drown their sorrows together, she thought.

The street with its row of neat terraced houses was relatively quiet in the sunshine. Kate paid off the cab, and walked up the path to the front door, exchanging a brief smile with the woman next door, who was planting some tubs.

She rang the bell, and waited, but there was no immediate reply.

Perhaps Louie really was physically ill, Kate thought, her brow creasing. She bent and called through the letterbox.

'Louie, it's me. Are you all right? Please open the door.'

'I don't think she's there.' The neighbour's head popped over the fence. 'I saw her going off in a taxi yesterday with a suitcase, and I haven't noticed her coming back.'

'You must be mistaken,' Kate said quickly. 'She's off sick. She rang to say so.'

'But I saw her.' The other woman bridled slightly. 'Clear as I'm seeing you now.' She paused. 'Maybe she's gone to a health farm,' she offered helpfully, then glanced at Kate and frowned. 'You don't look so good yourself, either. You've gone really white. Not going to faint, are you?'

No, Kate thought, biting her lip until she could taste blood. I'm not going to faint. Or scream. Or weep.

Aloud, she said, 'I'm sorry to have missed her. But I think I can guess where she's gone.' She thrust the roses and freesias she was carrying over the fence. 'Perhaps you'd like to have these.'

'Well, that's kind.' The woman accepted the bouquet doubtfully. 'Are you quite sure you don't want to keep them yourself?'

Kate's smile was like steel. 'They're not my favourite flowers.' *Or not any more, certainly.*

'Do you want me to tell her you called? When she comes back, that is,' the woman called after her.

'No, thanks.' Kate kept walking. 'I expect I'll see her before you do.'

There was a coffee shop in the next street. She ordered herself a black coffee and took it to a corner table. She needed a stimulant of some kind to alleviate the shock she'd just received. And she needed, too, to sit down before she fell.

She sat, watching the dark, fragrant liquid cool, while her mind went over and over the evidence. But no matter how she tried to load the equation she kept coming up with the same terrible answer.

Louie, she thought sickly. Louie—and Ryan.

It explained so much, of course, she realised, forcing herself to examine some of the conversations she'd had with both of them in the past week.

Remembering the dinner party. Coming into the

room, and finding them together. The look on Louie's face...

And she, fool that she was, standing up for Louie, and her forbidden love. Even defending her.

Ryan had tried to warn her. She could see that now.

She also understood, too late, why he had made love to her. To allay her suspicions, she thought, swallowing past the hard lump in her throat.

How they must have been laughing at her behind her back, she thought, anguished.

All desire to go to Yorkshire had left her. The last thing in the world she wanted was to see them together, and be confronted with the final confirmation of all her worst imaginings. Although she would have to face them some time.

Her husband. Her best friend. Her betrayers.

The coffee was bitter in her mouth but she swallowed it anyway, and left, thrusting the unwanted bottle of wine into a rubbish bin on the pavement.

I can't think what to do, said the toneless voice in her head as she walked. I can't go back to the flat—not yet. I have nothing—and no one... And I'm afraid to be alone.

They said the best place to hide was in a crowd, and that was what she would do. She'd go up West. Have a meal, whether she wanted it or not. Catch a film.

Because she wasn't ready to decide on her real next step. At the moment, she was in shock, but soon she would be angry, and she needed to deal with that before considering what options remained to her.

I want to make Ryan sorry, she thought, her hands curling painfully into fists. I want to see him suffer, as I am now—if that's possible. I—I want revenge.

She reached the junction with the main road, and paused, scanning the traffic for a cruising black cab.

When a hand fell on her shoulder, she nearly yelled with frights, spinning round to face the aggressor, her hand tightening on the strap of her bag.

'God, I'm sorry.' The would-be mugger spoke with penitence and real charm. 'I didn't mean to startle you like that.' He paused. 'I don't suppose you remember me.'

'Yes,' Kate said slowly. 'I remember you very well. You're Peter Henderson.'

He nodded. 'The wedding that wasn't. But which is going to happen next week instead.' He smiled. 'In a registry office with a few witnesses.'

'Just as you said,' Kate agreed with an effort. 'Well, I'm glad everything's worked out for the best.'

'So what are you doing in this neck of the woods? It's a bit far from home base, isn't it?'

I went to visit a friend.' Kate paused. 'Only she isn't there any more.'

'Then her loss is my gain.' His face was hopeful. 'Any chance of us having a drink before you dash devotedly home again?'

Kate looked up at him. She'd been aware of his attraction at their first meeting. Today, his City

clothes gave him extra distinction. And he was still
interested in her.

It occurred to her with sudden, icy clarity how her
revenge on Ryan could be achieved.

She stretched her dry lips into an approximation of
a smile.

'Thank you.' She said quietly. 'I—I'd really like
that.'

CHAPTER NINE

'WELL, this is marvellous. Here's to happy meetings.' Peter Henderson raised his glass, and Kate responded.

'I couldn't believe it when I saw you on that corner,' he went on. 'I called to you, but you seemed to be in another world.'

'I'm sorry.' Kate traced the stem of her wine glass with a finger. 'I've got a lot on my mind at the moment.'

He gave her a searching look. 'I really frightened you, didn't I? You still look a bit green about the gills.'

A reluctant laugh broke from her. 'Aren't you the flatterer?'

'Are you sure you're all right?'

'I'm certain.' She looked round her at the crowded wine bar. 'This is a nice place.'

'It's always been a favourite of mine.' He paused, then said abruptly, 'I've thought about you, you know. Wondered how you were getting along.'

Kate lowered her lashes. 'And I've thought about you.'

'Really?' He seemed so genuinely pleased that Kate felt a stab of conscience.

'And how's the famous writer?' he went on after another pause.

'Oh—he's away.' She looked down at the table.

'Really? Does that mean you don't have to rush home this evening—and you might be free to have dinner with me?'

'I'm sure you already have plans.' Kate spread her hands in deprecation.

'On the contrary, I'd be delighted if you'd agree to brighten up a lonely Monday evening. You can't turn me down a second time.'

She could hardly tell him she had no intention of turning him down, Kate thought ruefully. Or that her own plans didn't stop at dinner.

She laughed. 'Well, I was planning to open a very exciting tin...'

While he telephoned for a reservation, Kate went to the powder room.

She stared wonderingly at herself, reflected in the mirror over the basin. Saw the glitter in her eyes. The spots of colour burning in her face.

What am I doing? she asked herself in sudden bewilderment. What am I actually contemplating here?

But she already knew the answer to that. She'd been cheated on, and she was going to get her own back. It was all quite clear and perfectly simple.

Ryan was going to find out that he wasn't the only one with a significant other in his life. That the same sauce applied to goose and gander alike.

Besides, to all intents and purposes, her marriage

was over, thanks to Ryan, and she was now a free agent. A single woman again. And who was to say that Peter Henderson might not become a permanent fixture in her new life? she thought, tilting her chin defiantly.

Like many other woman, she had to start fashioning a new life out of the ruins of the old.

But I loved my old life, she thought with sudden desolation. I want it back.

But that decision, alas, was not solely hers to make, and Ryan had made another choice. The pain of it made her cringe inwardly, but, somehow, she had to surmount the trauma of his infidelity. Survive and go on, whatever the price.

Starting tonight, she had to convince herself that she was still worthwhile—even desirable, as Peter's eyes were already telling her.

That the loss of Ryan's love was not some black hole down which she was doomed to fall, screaming, through all eternity, however much it might feel like it.

She had her pride. Maybe it was all she had. So, she wasn't going to be the little woman waiting submissively to be told she was surplus to requirements.

She gave herself a fierce nod, and went back to rejoin her date.

'It's a new French restaurant,' Peter said in the cab. 'I've heard good reports about it.

Oh, God, Kate thought, her toes curling. Please—
not the Amaryllis.

And for once her prayer was answered.

The signboard outside said La Rivière, and Kate
found herself in a long, narrow room, with a plain
wood floor, and white walls enlivened by murals de-
picting scenes of some of France's great rivers.
Glancing round, she recognised instantly the turreted
grace of the Loire valley, the Île de la Cité on the
Seine, the sleepy Dordogne, and the mighty Rhône
reaching the bridge at Avignon.

The food, she discovered, was equally appealing.
They began with *pâté de campagne*, and moved on to
a rich meaty cassoulet, bursting with flavour.

He was surprisingly easy to talk to. He knew about
food and wine, and clearly enjoyed them, without being pretentious. He liked books, too, and was a regular
theatre-goer.

At one point, Kate found herself thinking, Ryan
would like him and had to pretend to retrieve her table
napkin in order to recover her composure.

She hadn't expected to be able to eat a thing, but
realised as the food was set in front of her that she
was actually ravenous.

Perhaps I'm going to be one of those people who
turns to the fridge in times of trouble, she thought
with a sigh, as she finished her last mouthful of cassoulet.

'Is something the matter?' Clearly, he didn't
miss much.

'Nothing at all,' she lied, smiling brilliantly at him. 'I was just thinking what a marvellous place this is. I must tell...' She halted abruptly.

'Tell whom?' Peter prompted. 'Your husband?'

'No.' She flushed dully. 'I was going to say— Louie, my business partner.'

'What stopped you?'

She looked down at the table. 'Because I don't think the partnership will last much longer. I—I imagine we'll be folding the company.'

'That's a shame.' He frowned slightly. 'Won't you feel lost without it?'

A month—a week—twenty-four hours ago even— she'd have said yes and meant it. Now, in the light of all the greater losses she'd suffered, she shrugged. 'Not any more.'

'You surprise me,' he said lightly. 'I had you down as one of the new female entrepreneurs who have it all, dividing your time effortlessly between marriage and being Businesswoman of the Year.'

'There's nothing effortless about being married, believe me.' The bitterness overflowed before she could prevent it.

'But it must have its compensations, otherwise people would give it up as a bad job.' He passed her a dessert menu. 'The *tarte tatin* is excellent,' he added.

She shook her head. 'I really couldn't eat another thing.'

'Fine,' he said equably. 'My flat isn't far from here. I could offer you coffee, and a good Armagnac.'

So, this was it, she thought, swallowing. Cards on the table time. She was so out of touch with current courting rituals that she hadn't even seen it coming. And, somehow, she'd expected him to be rather more subtle, too, and she felt oddly disappointed.

But she didn't let it show. She made herself smile straight into his eyes. 'That would be—' she held the pause quite deliberately '—very nice.'

And no marks for subtlety there either, she added under her breath.

He lived on the third floor of a handsome red-brick block. The flat was spacious, its furniture a comfortable mix of the up-to-date with some antique pieces which she guessed had come from his family.

While he was busy in the kitchen, she wandered round, her untouched brandy glass in her hand, looking at things without really seeing them. Pausing at the window, she parted the long green drapes a fraction, staring out into the gathering darkness.

Someone had once said that revenge was a dish best eaten cold, and it must be true because she felt as if she'd been turned to ice.

'Come and have some coffee.' Peter had returned, and was setting a tray on the low table in front of the sofa.

Biting her lip, she joined him, perching self-consciously on the edge of the deep cushions, watching him fill tall porcelain beakers from the cafetière, telling herself he'd hardly reach out and grab her if she was holding a cup of scalding liquid.

She took the beaker he handed her with a murmured word of thanks, casting round in her mind for
something else to say—something that would signal
her availability to him—and convince her that this
was what she wanted.

But she couldn't think of a thing.

Maybe it would be better if he grabbed her after
all. Made the decision, and all the running too.

When he took the beaker from her hand and set it
back on the table, she did not resist, although she felt
her throat close in fright. Instead, she allowed him to
turn her gently to face him. His lips as they touched
hers were gentle too, almost tentative. They didn't
threaten a thing, and she closed her eyes, trying desperately to summon up a response—to feel something
other than totally numb—and failing.

All she could think of was Ryan, and the way her
body had blossomed joyously and urgently the first
time he had touched her hand.

The only man she had ever loved. The only man
she had ever really wanted. And nothing could change
that.

Peter said very softly, 'Ah.' Then let her go, and
reached instead for his coffee. There was a silence.

Eventually, 'What are you doing here, Kate?' His
voice was still quiet.

She took a hasty sip of her own coffee, burning her
mouth in the process. 'You invited me...'

'But I didn't expect you to accept,' he said slowly.
'You're married, Kate.'

'What difference does that make?' she demanded defensively.

'A hell of a lot, I'd have said. Especially to someone like you.' Peter shook his head. 'You've been like a cat on hot bricks all night. In fact, you're so brittle that if I really laid a hand on you you'd probably break.'

She tried to force a smile. 'You could always try—and find out.'

He shook his head again, slowly and regretfully. 'I don't think so. And it isn't because I don't want to. It's because I know your heart isn't in this.' He paused. Sighed. 'But mine could be, and I don't want it damaged.'

She put the beaker carefully back on the tray. 'I—see.'

'No, you don't, because I hardly do myself. I only know this can't happen, and I was a fool to think it might.' He gave her a fleeting, twisted smile. 'Now, drink your coffee, and the Armagnac because you look as if you need it, then I'll take you home.'

She said stiffly, 'There's no need for that.'

'Yes, there is.' The contradiction was firm. 'Because in another time, another place, another dimension, this could have worked for us.' He paused. 'As it is, I feel that I'm caught up in something that's going on in your life, and I'm not prepared to take advantage of your unhappiness.'

Kate bent her head. 'I'm so ashamed.' Her voice

sounded stifled. 'I thought I could—I meant to—but I can't. I'm—so sorry…'

'I know,' he said. 'And it's all right.' He hesitated. 'Do you want to talk about what's really happening?'

She shook her head. A slow, scalding tear crept down her face. 'I can't do that either.'

'Ah, well.' Peter's tone was philosophical. 'Let's just say we had a terrific meal together, and leave it at that.'

Her mouth trembled into a smile. 'You are such a truly nice man. I just wish…'

'No, you don't.' He pulled a face. 'That'll teach me to go poaching on someone else's preserves.'

They didn't talk much during the cab ride home.

'Will you be all right?' Peter asked as he took her to the lift.

No, Kate thought. But at least I haven't made a bad situation worse.

She lifted her chin. 'I'll be fine. And—thank you for being so understanding.'

'They tell me it's my best feature.' His lips brushed her cheek, then he was gone.

Kate closed the door behind her, and stood for a moment, leaning against its panels, listening to the silence, as a sigh shook her body.

On a scale of one to ten, the last forty-eight hours registered minus fifty or less, she thought, wincing.

And her behaviour this evening didn't bear consideration.

Isn't it enough to be hurt and angry? she derided herself. Do I have to go stark, staring mad as well? What the hell did I think I was doing?

If Peter Henderson had been a different kind of man, she could have been in real trouble.

A glance towards the answering machine told her that no messages had been logged. But then, what did she expect?

Listlessly, she went into the kitchen, and made herself some herbal tea. It might calm her—help her to sleep, she thought as she sipped it. It might even stop her thinking.

She couldn't face another night on the sofa. Besides, she had to start getting used to the empty place in the bed, she told herself as she showered and put on her nightgown.

But that was easier said than done. She found she was lying, staring into the darkness, trying to come to terms with a future that did not include Ryan.

And I thought we were so happy, she derided herself. I thought we had it all. Careers, lifestyle, fulfilment.

And yet, looking back, she realised that Ryan's enthusiasm for the outward trappings of their success had always been muted.

She had chosen their apartment, and he'd gone along with her choice. As he'd said, with a shrug, he could write anywhere. But she could see now that he'd never regarded it as home, in the same way as their old basement flat.

I wanted prestige—to send out signals to the world, she thought. Because I was happy, I presumed Ryan would be contented as well. Only, he wasn't. He wanted a very different kind of life—the one we'd always talked about—and I still wanted that, in a way. But there was so much else going on, it seemed easier to postpone it. To think about it later. To tell myself there was all the time in the world.

But—he got tired of waiting.

She wondered how long it would have taken her to realise what was going on without that anonymous letter, which, she supposed, wincing, Louie must have sent.

When had their affair actually begun? It was small comfort to know that they had both tried to finish it at some point. And had Louie even been the first?

Shuddering, Kate rolled over, burying her face in the pillow. Ryan's pillow, she thought as she breathed the faint scent of his cologne. Another trace of his presence which she would have to eradicate if she was to find any piece of mind.

She sat up abruptly, pushing the pillow off the bed altogether.

'I can't stay here,' she said aloud into the darkness. 'I can't bear the associations. At least, not yet. And I can't just wait here for him to return and break the news either. It will be easier—simpler for both of us if I've already moved out. No explanations—no excuses—just a clean break.

Tomorrow, she'd find herself a bed-sitter. Just

somewhere to stay until she could make some real plans.

It wasn't just her life with Ryan that was going to be dismantled. It was the business too. Her future livelihood. She'd have to prepare a business forecast, raise a loan, and buy Louie out. Find new premises too. Somewhere without memories.

'I'll start tomorrow,' she vowed, lying down and resolutely closing her eyes.

She woke to grey skies and rain, which seemed wholly appropriate under the circumstances. Weather to suit her mood, she thought, pouring orange juice.

'Louie's still off,' Debbie reported plaintively as she got into the office.

'She—may not be back for a while.' Kate spoke carefully. 'We'll have to cope.'

It was another busy morning, with the telephone ringing constantly. Kate was just completing an estimate when a call came in on her direct line.

'Yes,' she said absently, her mind on the figures in front of her.

'Kate, dear, it's Mary.' Her mother-in-law's voice sounded diffident. 'Sally and I are in town to do some shopping. I know it's short notice, but could you manage to get away for lunch?' She paused. 'There's something we need to discuss.'

Kate swallowed. 'Is—there?' she said woodenly.

'I think so.' Mary Lassiter hesitated. 'I've booked a table at Wallaces for one-thirty.' She gave a little awkward laugh. 'I hope that's not too staid and traditional for you.'

'No,' Kate said quietly. 'I—I'll look forward to seeing you.'

She replaced the receiver, and looked back at the VDU screen, but the figures were dancing meaninglessly in front of her.

She took a deep breath. Surely Ryan hadn't delegated his mother to break the news to her? Was his feeling of guilt so immense that he couldn't bring himself to face up to her in person? she asked herself hotly, before remembering her own intention to avoid him by moving out of the flat.

So, she could tell Mrs Lassiter that her intervention was unnecessary. That she already knew all there was to know, and was making her plans accordingly.

And his mother could tell Ryan.

Wallaces had always been popular with her parents-in-law, Kate recalled, as her cab stopped outside its imposing frontage. What she still couldn't understand was why she'd agreed to come, she thought, without pleasure. Sheltering under her umbrella, she paid the driver, then ducked under the smart dark green awning.

It was, indeed, a conventional restaurant, serving basic English food. At lunchtime, to supplement the normal menu, a covered trolley containing the roast joint of the day was wheeled between the tables.

Mrs Lassiter and Sally were already in their seats.

As Kate approached, her mother-in-law got to her feet, but Sally stayed where she was.

'Kate, dear. It seems ages since we saw you.' There was a touch of constraint in Mrs Lassiter's voice, but the kiss she bestowed on Kate's cheek held its usual warmth.

Then she stood back and regarded her a mite critically. 'You've lost weight. I hope you're not on one of those wretched diets.'

'I think it might possibly be stress,' Kate said levelly. Hello, Sally.'

'Hi.' Sally gave her an uncertain look.

'We're drinking mineral water,' Mrs Lassiter said, as she resumed her seat. 'But if you'd like something stronger, go ahead.'

'Do you think I need it?' Kate's smile was tight-lipped. 'Can I say, I know why you've asked me here? What you have to tell me.'

'You do?' Mrs Lassiter looked momentarily blank, then rallied. 'Well, that's all right, then, isn't it—and we can just have a pleasant lunch…'

'Actually, it's not all right.' Sally, suddenly flushed, leaned forward, her voice low and angry. 'A word of congratulation might be nice—or even an enquiry about how I'm feeling. But that's too much to hope for, of course. Ever since you married Ryan, we've all had to tiptoe round your finer feelings—make sure we didn't upset you. Well, I don't care any more. I think you're a self-centred bitch.'

Kate's brows snapped together incredulously. 'Now just a minute…'

'I haven't finished.' Sally took a deep, fierce breath. 'As it happens, I love my husband, and I love my babies. I get more fulfilment from them than I ever did from my career. Whatever you may think, I'm happy. So can we dispense with the pitying looks, and critical remarks, please?'

Understanding hit Kate like a sledgehammer. 'My God,' she said, slowly. 'Sally—you're having another baby.'

'I already know that,' her sister-in-law retorted. 'And so does everyone in the family, barring you. But you mustn't be told in case you think you're being got at again, and you start giving my poor bloody brother another hard time.'

'That was my fault,' Mrs Lassiter said remorsefully. 'I was tactless and interfering—oh, all those things that I most despise in other mothers-in-law. I don't blame Kate for being angry.'

Kate stared at them both. 'That day I came down to lunch. That was what it was all about?'

Sally looked right back at her, her eyes challenging. 'We'd arranged a little celebration, but we couldn't have it with you there, just in case you thought we were rubbing salt into the wound. Dropping hints.'

'But I wouldn't,' Kate protested.

'Really?' The other girl's tone was sceptical. 'It didn't seem to take much to put your back up. And I probably wouldn't be telling you about it now except that I'll be starting to show soon.'

'Sally,' her mother said sharply. 'That's quite enough.'

Kate drew a deep breath. 'A moment ago, you called me a self-centred bitch. It seems an apt description. I'm sorry you didn't feel you could let me in on such an important secret before now. I—I'm really happy for you, Sally.'

Mrs Lassiter's brow was furrowed. 'Have you really only just guessed, dear? From what you said just now—'

'Oh, that was something else,' Kate interrupted swiftly. 'And it's really not important.' She couldn't spoil the moment by telling them that she and Ryan were splitting up. And they'd find out soon enough anyway, she reminded herself unhappily.

She hurried into speech again. 'By the way, lunch is on me.' She gave Sally an awkward smile. 'Can you manage some champagne, or will the baby object?'

Her sister-in-law's face was marginally softer. 'I don't suppose one glass will hurt. At least I've stopped throwing up now. I don't know who called it morning sickness, but it used to hit me any hour out of the twenty-four, short, sharp and very unpleasant.'

She put out a hand and touched Kate's sleeve. 'Thanks, Kate. And I'm sorry I sounded off at you. Put it down to hormonal imbalance.' She gave her a searching look. 'Are you all right? You suddenly look as if you've been poleaxed. Was it something I said?'

'No,' Kate forced through dry lips. 'I suddenly remembered something I'd completely overlooked, that's all.' She looked round for the waiter. 'Are we ready to order?'

On the surface, she was the life and soul of the party, laughing, talking, and making extravagant toasts to Sally and the baby.

While all the time a voice in her head was whispering, It can't be true. It was only a tummy bug. That was all. It can't be anything else. It just can't. Not now. Not ever.

And, with that realisation, she wanted to put her head down on the table and sob her heart out.

CHAPTER TEN

'WELL, I'm delighted to tell you that you're quite correct.' Dr Hamell gave her patient a gentle smile. 'Did you really not guess you were pregnant, Mrs Lassiter?'

Kate shook her head. 'Not until today when my sister-in-law was talking.' She stared back at the doctor. 'But I'm on the pill.'

'Which isn't infallible.' Dr Hamell doodled on the pad in front of her. 'Especially if you've had any kind of gastric upset in the last month or so. Have you?'

Kate nodded. 'Even so, I seem to have lost weight, not gained it.'

'Well, that also can happen in the early stages, but you'll soon make up for it. Surely you realised that you'd missed a period?'

Kate swallowed. 'I—just didn't notice,' she mumbled. 'I've had a great deal on my mind lately. Been under a lot of stress.'

'Well, that can stop at once,' the doctor said with mock severity. 'I'd like you to have a word with the practice nutritionist, and also make another appointment to see me next week when you've recovered from the shock.' She paused. 'I suppose you want to dash home and tell your husband.'

167

'He isn't there.' Kate's mouth was desert-dry. 'He's away, lecturing.'

'Well, it will be a wonderful homecoming surprise for him.'

If only, thought Kate, emerging into the street, where a watery sun was trying to break through the clouds.

As soon as lunch was finished, she'd made some random excuse and gone straight to the medical centre where she and Ryan were registered, and asked for an emergency appointment.

I have to know, she'd told herself as she sat in the waiting room.

Well, now she did know, and a lot of good it had done her.

At any other time, she'd have been dancing down the street. Now, her feet were like lead, and she felt cold and sick with apprehension.

In a matter of hours, she'd lost her husband, her friend and business partner, and acquired single parenthood. It was hardly a bargain, she thought bitterly.

But recriminations were pointless. Now, she had some hard thinking and even more difficult decisions to make.

She would go back to the office and clear her desk, and tell Debbie she was having a couple of days off. And then she'd find some kind of sanctuary while she tried to get her head together.

She met Debbie on the stairs. 'Louie's back,' the

younger girl threw at her as she dashed past. 'And we're out of coffee.'

For a moment, Kate stood where she was, her hands clenching into fists at her sides as she mustered her defences. Then, lifting her chin, she climbed the remaining steps and pushed open the door.

Louie was in the reception area, her face intent as she arranged a mass of long-stemmed yellow roses in the company's one and only vase.

'Hi.' She tried to sound nonchalant. 'Aren't these beautiful? They're actually for you, but I thought you wouldn't mind if I looked after them.'

'Help yourself,' Kate said quietly. *You've taken everything else in my life, so what's a bunch of flowers?* Aloud, she went on, 'I wasn't expecting to see you.'

'Or I to be here.' Louie bit her lip. 'I'm sorry I fibbed about being ill. Mrs Ransom said you'd called with flowers. I—I felt awful.'

'Because you'd been found out?' Kate asked levelly. 'Or did you expect your plan to remain a big secret?'

Louie winced. 'I don't know what I expected. I didn't even start to think until I got to Heathrow, and that was when I realised I couldn't go through with it.' She threw her head back. 'That Ryan was right, after all. That it was over, and I should let it rest.' Her brows snapped together. 'Kate—are you all right? You look terrible.'

'How am I supposed to look—hearing you talk

about him like that?' Kate demanded harshly. 'You think because it's in the past it doesn't matter any more? If so, you're as wrong as can be.'

Louie stared at her, aghast. 'But you encouraged me. You said you'd be on my side, whatever. I didn't know Joe's marriage was that important to you.'

'Joe?' It was Kate's turn to stare. 'You mean Joe Hartley? What's he got to do with it?'

'Joe and I were seeing each other for nearly a year,' Louie said tightly. 'Eventually he decided to take the transfer to New York, and see if he could put his marriage back together. Try for a baby. The whole works. Two days ago, I decided to follow. To try and get him back.' Her hands were clasped tautly together. 'I—I thought you knew. That Ryan must have told you.'

Kate shook here head numbly. 'No, he never said a word.'

'He's been—very forbearing.' Louie's lips twisted wryly. 'Especially as I knew he disapproved like hell.' She paused. 'We met at your flat—at that New Year drinks party, remember—when his wife had a cold and didn't come.'

'Yes,' Kate said shakily. 'I remember.' She could even recall Louie and Joe talking together in a corner, their heads close together. Recall her pleasure in seeing them enjoy each other's company. Liking her friends to be friends.

She drew a deep breath. 'My God, just how dumb can anyone be?'

'Dumb I can understand, but why so angry?' Louie gave her an uncertain look. 'Honest to God, Katie, just now you looked as if you hated me. As if I was the scum of the earth. And I didn't *do* anything.'

'So where have you been?' Kate was still wary.

Louie sighed. 'After I cancelled my plane ticket, I holed up at one of the airport hotels—lived on room service. I cried a bit, and got angry with myself.' She pulled a wry face. 'The usual things. I know it was stupid, and it left you in the lurch, but I just needed to—bury the past in my own way. I was sure you'd understand.'

'I don't think I understand very much at all—even now,' Kate admitted wearily. 'I'm sorry, Lou. I've clearly got hold of the wrong end of all kinds of sticks. I think I need to get away myself, and cry and be angry.'

Louie's eyes were compassionate. 'You look as if you could do with a rest,' she agreed. 'What does Ryan think?'

'Ryan's not around.' Somehow she managed to keep her voice from wobbling. 'He's up in the north, lecturing.'

With someone I thought was you, and though I'm so glad to be wrong it doesn't make the actual situation any better.

In fact, she realised, Louie's revelation had thrown everything back into the melting pot.

'So, he's away. I see.' There was an odd note in Louie's voice. 'Kate—tell me to mind my own business if you want, but is everything all right with you and Ryan?'

Kate lifted her chin, her heart thumping violently. 'What makes you ask?'

Louie had confided in Ryan, she thought. Perhaps there'd been some kind of reciprocal arrangement. Maybe Louie had even been asked to break the news to her.

However, Louie was directing a significant glance towards the bowl of yellow roses. 'These for one thing. They were delivered in person half an hour ago by a tall blond job, drop-dead gorgeous, with voice and smile to match. Said his name was Peter and he was calling by to make sure you were all right.' She gave Kate a straight look. 'Well—are you?'

'I shall be,' Kate said steadily. 'And—Peter—the flowers—aren't what you think. He—he's just a friend.'

Louie sighed. 'I should have such friends,' she muttered. 'I wish I'd said you were on the danger list, then he might have called again.'

In spite of her inner turmoil, Kate felt a reluctant grin fight its way to the surface.

'Lou, you're the limit.' She paused. 'And I need a favour—a couple of days off, no questions asked.' She saw her friend's eyebrows snap together and added hastily, 'And it has nothing to do with Peter Henderson, I swear.'

Louie's forehead was still furrowed. 'Are you sure I can't help?'

'Not right now.' Kate's throat tightened. 'But maybe in the future…'

Louie hugged her with sudden fierceness. 'I can't begin to guess what's going on,' she whispered. 'But take all the time you need.'

It was evening by the time Kate reached Allengarth. She had driven steadily, concentrating doggedly on the traffic sharing the motorway with her, calming herself with her favourite tapes played over and over again. Not letting herself think about what might face her at the end of the journey.

Simply allowing herself to acknowledge that she was thankful the uncertainty would be over soon. And that knowing the whole truth at last could only be a relief.

It was only a small village, sheltering in the Dales, a cluster of sturdy grey stone houses around a church and a chapel. There was a pub too, with a bed and breakfast sign propped in a window.

Kate went in and booked herself a room. Under the circumstances, she could hardly expect to stay at the Centre, she reasoned. And it was unlikely she would feel like making an immediate return journey to London either.

The way to the Centre was clearly sign-posted, so Kate left her car in the parking area at the rear of the pub, and walked the half mile out of the village.

The air was cool and clean, and she drew it deeply into her lungs. As she reached the Centre's gates, she hesitated momentarily, then squared her shoulders and went up the broad drive.

There were lights on in the building ahead. Kate let herself in through the double glass doors, and stood looking around. There was a reception desk on the right, and through an open door she could see a bar area with groups of people gathered, talking. She went over and looked in, but couldn't sight Ryan.

The obvious thing was to ask at Reception, but she was reluctant to do this.

After all, she thought painfully, she'd driven a lot of miles to catch him unawares.

She glanced around, and saw on one of the walls an enormous pinboard covered in notices. Most of them were the usual kind of thing—a plan of the building, a copy of the programme, instructions about mealtimes and fire alarms. But there was also a list of all the delegates attending the convention—and their room numbers.

Scanning it, she saw that Ryan was occupying the Main Suite on Floor One.

Kate swallowed, her fingers closing convulsively round the strap of her bag. The time had come, and there was nothing she could do to turn back the clock to happier days.

She found the suite without difficulty, its door facing her at the end of a long corridor. There was a notice attached to the handle, stating 'Please do not disturb'.

I bet, thought Kate, bitterness clenching her throat.

She was about to knock when impulse prompted her to try the door instead, and, to her surprise, it opened at once.

She flung it wide, hearing it bang as it knocked against some piece of occasional furniture inside, and marched in.

She was aware of movement. Of heads turning. But the only person in the room she saw was Ryan.

He had risen to his feet, and was looking at her, head thrown slightly back, his eyes hooded.

He said quietly, 'Hello, Kate.'

She had planned it all on the walk here. She was going to be dignified—civilised. She was not going to break down, or make a scene.

But at the sight of him—his self-possession when she was falling apart—something exploded in her head.

Her voice when it emerged was on the edge of a scream.

'Don't you dare say "Hello" to me. Don't you bloody dare. I'm pregnant, do you hear me? Pregnant.'

There was a stunned silence, then hesitantly some-one began to clap. Others joined in, the applause hammering in her ears, alerting her consciousness. She was in a sitting room, she realised, suddenly becoming aware of a dozen chairs set in a semicircle, of surprised smiling faces turned towards her.

Only Ryan's face remained serious, almost watch-ful. He said quietly, 'As you can gather, ladies and gentlemen, this is not part of the course.' He waited for the brief ripple of laughter to die down, then added, 'Maybe we could resume tomorrow.'

There was a murmur of acquiescence. People began to rise, moving chairs back to the wall, collecting papers, picking up briefcases, as Ryan began ushering them to the door.

Kate, standing as if she'd been turned to stone, could feel their eyes upon her. Could sense the interest, the half-whispered comments.

But where was the girl she'd come to see? Certainly, not among this group. The only woman present had reached early middle age by her reckoning.

There was another door in the far wall. Kate crossed to it, threw it open, and went in. The room beyond was spacious, with fitted wardrobes and chests of drawers, and a large double bed covered by a handsome patchwork quilt. It was also empty.

Kate marched over to the wardrobes, and pulled open the doors. In the first, she found Ryan's clothes—jeans, a pair of trousers, shirts, and his favourite jacket—hanging there in splendid if lonely isolation. The others contained nothing at all.

In one of the chests of drawers, she came upon his socks and underwear. But there were no signs anywhere of the feminine occupation that she'd expected.

'I'd just been talking to them about dramatic openings,' Ryan said laconically from the doorway. 'Your arrival couldn't have been more timely.'

'Don't,' she said between her teeth, 'just don't you laugh at me, you bastard.'

'Do you see me looking even remotely amused?'

She couldn't pretend that she did. His face looked as if it had been hacked from granite, his mouth grim, the lines beside it deeply scored.

He said quietly, 'How long have you known—about the baby?'

'I found out today.'

'And came straight to accuse me.' It was a statement rather than a question. 'Also, no doubt, to receive my apology for having thrown a spanner into the works of your brilliant career. Well, you'll wait a long time for that, Katie.'

Kate's head was whirling. She'd arrived to confront him and now, it seemed, the tables had been turned in some way, and she was in the wrong.

Her lips parted in denial but Ryan cut across her. 'So what happens next? Do we move to an even bigger and better flat, hire a nanny, and watch our lives eventually resume their normal pattern after this minor disruption?'

Kate lifted her chin. 'I didn't come to discuss any of that. I—I'm not sure I actually meant to mention the baby.'

'Now that I can believe.' His tone was bitter. He gestured towards the open drawer. 'Looking for something?'

'I was, but you seem to have disposed of the evidence. Is that something your thriller writing has taught you?'

'It's certainly taught me that things are not always what they seem.' He detached himself from the doorway, and walked across to her. 'So, what have you come here for—if not to tell me I'm going to be a father.'

'Because you're having an affair. And I want to face you with it. To see her.' She slammed the drawer shut. 'Don't pretend to me, Ryan. I—I know. I've known for weeks.'

He sat down on the edge of the bed. His eyes never left her face. 'How did you find out about her?'

So, he wasn't even going to attempt a denial. Pain twisted in her throat. She said huskily, 'I had a letter—a beastly anonymous thing.'

'May I see it?'

Kate shook her head violently. 'I tore it up. Then I burnt the bits.'

'Pretty comprehensive treatment,' Ryan acknowledged drily, after a pause. 'Can you remember what it said?'

'Just that you loved another woman.' She swallowed a sob. 'And it was signed "A Friend". That was the worst thing of all. She may be your woman, but don't you think that's pretty disgusting, Ryan?'

'Why have you never mentioned this letter before—as it clearly made such an impression on you?'

'Wasn't that what it was intended to do? Or didn't you know it had been written?'

'Yes,' he said, and there was an odd note in his voice. 'I knew. But it didn't produce the effect I expected.'

'Did you hope I'd leave—walk out on you, leaving the way clear for her?'

'On the contrary, I thought you'd confront me with the bloody thing. Fly at me—scream—hit me, even. Demand to know what was going on.'

'What good would that have done?' She lifted her chin. 'I—I'm not going to make a scene even now. I've made enough of a fool of myself on past occasions. All I came for was proof.'

'Why did you think you'd find it here?'

'Because she came with you. You booked her in as your wife. That's why they gave you this suite.'

He shook his head. 'Wrong, Katie. I booked you in as my wife. Although I wasn't altogether sure you'd come. I just—prayed that you would. I relied on you caring enough to follow me.'

'Why? Because your other woman let you down?'

He said gently. 'You're my other woman, Katie. You, and no one else. There never has been—and there never will be anyone. Only you.'

Her lips parted in bewilderment. 'But the letter...'

'I wrote it,' he said. He reached up and took her hands, drawing her down on the bed beside him. She realised he was shaking.

'I'm not proud of it,' he went on. 'But I was desperate, and I couldn't think what else to do. I could see you walking away down this bright tunnel—your eyes fixed on a different horizon—getting further away from me, and the girl I married, with every day that passed.'

He shook his head. 'You will never know how lonely I was. How frightened. Do you realise whole days went by when we barely spoke? Whole weekends passed, and I never saw you. All our dreams and plans seemed to have been sidelined. And I'd watched Joe go through the same kind of thing in his marriage, and nearly lose everything.'

He drew a ragged breath. 'I thought I was losing you, Katie, and I couldn't bear it.'

He paused. 'I needed to know if you could bear to lose me. I always told you I was a gambler—and this time I risked everything.'

There was a silence. Then, 'I don't believe you.' Her voice cracked. 'How could you do such a thing?'

'I needed a reaction from you.' Ryan said with quiet intensity. 'I suppose, God help me, that I wanted you to fight for me—to show that you cared. That, somehow, against all the odds, you still shared our dream.'

He lifted her hands and held them against his heart.

'I love you, Kate—more than you'll ever know. I'd have done all this and more to win you back to me. If you can't forgive me for it—that's something I'll learn to endure somehow. But I had to try.'

'You let me go through all that?' She was shaking now. 'Follow you round London—everywhere…?'

He groaned. 'I swear I never thought it would get

that far. If you'd challenged me at any point, I'd have told you the truth at once. I expected we'd have one almighty blow-up—make or break time. I was prepared for that. But whichever way it turned out—I still had to know.'

He took her face tenderly in his hands, staring into her eyes, his own hazel gaze anguished. 'I wouldn't blame you if you hated me. But you did follow me, Katie. You're here now where you belong. Doesn't that, surely, mean that you care? That we have something together that's worth fighting for?'

His face was pleading—vulnerable. She heard the uncertainty in his tone—the self-blame.

And suddenly she saw their marriage as he had seen it. And, in that moment, realised how close to the brink they had come. How easy it could have been to slide into the abyss.

We were growing apart, she thought with shock. I should have realised when Peter Henderson asked me to have dinner with him that first time, and I was actually tempted.

Or perhaps I did know, and that's what sent me racing home. Maybe I sensed the danger too.

In the stillness, she heard him whisper her name.

'I care.' Her voice broke. 'Oh, Ryan, I've been so miserable—so utterly wretched.' She leaned forward, her lips trembling, clumsy as they found his, her hands clinging to his shoulders. 'I thought you didn't want me any more.'

'It was never that, my darling.' He held her close.

'But it seemed to me that even making love had drifted into a routine. And that a period of abstinence might do us both some good.'

He groaned. 'Although turning away from you was the worst thing I've ever had to do. Sometimes I was so crazy for you, I didn't dare come to bed.' Something like the old grin touched his mouth. 'But I knew my resolve couldn't last for ever. And the other night it broke, with spectacular results.'

Kate kissed him again, more lingeringly. 'I remember it well. But why did you walk away from me in the morning—when I wanted to come here with you? Why didn't you explain it all to me then?'

He was silent for a moment. 'I suppose I was afraid that bed might be the only place where we ever came to terms,' he said at last. 'And I wanted our marriage to work on every level. And also because I wasn't coming straight to Yorkshire. I made a slight detour on the way.'

'Oh?' Kate stiffened slightly in his arms.

Ryan nodded, slightly shamefaced. 'I have another confession to make. I've been house-hunting. I know how you feel about the flat, but I'm homesick for grass and trees and air that you can breathe, Katie. I want some space around me, and my own land to walk on. And there's Algy. He was bought for me originally, but I've never had anywhere to keep him.'

He paused. 'However, I realise you may not feel the same, so I thought—I hoped we could compromise.' He sounded anxious. 'Keep the flat on as well. Divide our time between the two somehow.'

She touched his face tenderly with her hand. 'I think the baby would much prefer the countryside. And I want to share our dream again too.' She shook her head. 'I knew something was missing. I just didn't know how to get it back.'

'But your work, Katie. The company. I know how much it means to you. And I want you to have it still.'

'I can work from home,' she said. 'Plenty of other women do. Although we'll need separate offices,' she added, crinkling her brow thoughtfully. 'Do I take it your detour was a success? That you've found somewhere?'

He nodded. 'It has real possibilities.' His voice was eager. 'It has a big garden, and an orchard, although the property itself needs some work. But the couple who own it have just celebrated their golden wedding, and they say it's a house for happiness...' He stopped abruptly. 'My God, does that sound ridiculously sentimental?'

'Not,' she said, 'to me.' For the first time in weeks, she felt totally at peace with herself, aware of tiny tendrils of hope and joy uncurling deep inside her. Putting out strong shoots, she thought. And smiled. 'Will Algy like the baby?'

'Bassets are terrific with kids,' Ryan assured her, then paused again, his face altering. 'My God, it's just occurred to me. The other night, when we made love—was it safe? Could we have hurt the baby?'

'The baby,' Kate told him softly, 'is just going to have to accustom itself. Starting now.'

Taking her time, she began to unbutton his shirt.

There was laughter in his voice. 'Does this mean you forgive me?'

'It might.' Kate pushed him gently back on the bed, and began to trail small kisses down his chest. 'As long as you're prepared to make full amends.'

'I shall devote the rest of my life to doing just that.' He drew her down to him, his mouth warm with promise as it caressed hers. The touch of his hands sure and knowing as he freed her from her clothes.

'Welcome back, Katie,' he whispered, as they came together in a sweet and tender giving. 'My wife—my only love. Welcome back.'

EPILOGUE

'I'LL never forgive Louie for this,' Kate said wrathfully, as she struggled with the zip on the hyacinth-blue wool dress. 'Couldn't she have waited a few more weeks to get married?'

'Let me do that.' Ryan came over to her, closed the zip, fastened the hook and eye, and bent to kiss the curve of her neck. 'Besides, would anything have stopped us?'

'I suppose not.' Kate ran her hands over her bump. 'Just look at me. If I had a basket to carry, I'd be the image of a hot-air balloon. It will serve Louie and Peter right if I go into labour in the middle of the ceremony.'

'You look beautiful.' Smiling, Ryan rested his chin on her shoulder. 'The title "matron of honour" has never been more richly deserved.

'And once the wedding's over,' he went on more sternly, 'you're going to take it easy. Moving house, and organizing your best friend's reception, is not what a pregnant lady should be doing.'

'I feel fine,' she assured him. 'And once I saw the house I wanted to be in it immediately. And I didn't do any actual lifting,' she added coaxingly.

185

'Damned right,' Ryan said with emphasis as he turned away to put on his coat.

'And I had to do the reception,' she went on. 'After all, Special Occasions brought them together.'

Or at least gave Peter the excuse he needed to call back and meet Louie again, she thought with satisfaction. Nature had seen to the rest, and had wasted no time about it.

'Fate can be really terrific sometimes,' she mused aloud. 'Have you ever met two people so happy—or so completely suited?'

'Oh, I can think of one other couple,' Ryan returned, clasping her fingers as they walked together down the curving flight of honey-coloured wood stairs.

Algy was sitting in his basket in the hall, looking glum, with something white and lacy dangling from his jowls.

'Oh, God,' Kate said wearily. 'He's got another of my bras. Why does he do this?'

'He hates us going out and leaving him, so he takes something to remember us by.'

'Well, he can't go with us. Not after his behaviour at Sally's christening party. Half my new nephew's cake had gone before we caught him,' Kate said severely. 'And why can't he pinch your stuff for a change?' She bent and stroked the basset's wrinkled forehead. 'At this rate, I'll have no underwear left.'

'A dog after my own heart,' Ryan murmured, dodging the mock blow she aimed at him. 'Wait here, darling, while I bring the car round. It's too cold for you to stand about outside.'

Left to herself, Kate wandered into the drawing room, and stood looking out of the window. Patches of last night's frost still silvered the lawn, and only the most resolute leaves still clung to the tree branches.

Before too long it would be Christmas—their first in their new home—and then, in the new year, their baby would be born.

Kate laid a protective hand on her tummy, feeling the child kick.

Our significant other, she thought with satisfaction. And went to join her husband.

If you enjoyed what you just read,
then we've got an offer you can't resist!

Take 2 bestselling love stories FREE!

Plus get a FREE surprise gift!

Clip this page and mail it to Harlequin Reader Service®

IN U.S.A.	IN CANADA
3010 Walden Ave.	P.O. Box 609
P.O. Box 1867	Fort Erie, Ontario
Buffalo, N.Y. 14240-1867	L2A 5X3

YES! Please send me 2 free Harlequin Presents® novels and my free surprise gift. Then send me 6 brand-new novels every month, which I will receive months before they're available in stores. In the U.S.A., bill me at the bargain price of $3.12 plus 25¢ delivery per book and applicable sales tax, if any*. In Canada, bill me at the bargain price of $3.49 plus 25¢ delivery per book and applicable taxes**. That's the complete price and a savings of over 10% off the cover prices—what a great deal! I understand that accepting the 2 free books and gift places me under no obligation ever to buy any books. I can always return a shipment and cancel at any time. Even if I never buy another book from Harlequin, the 2 free books and gift are mine to keep forever. So why not take us up on our invitation. You'll be glad you did!

106 HEN CNER
306 HEN CNES

Name	(PLEASE PRINT)	
Address	Apt.#	
City	State/Prov.	Zip/Postal Code

* Terms and prices subject to change without notice. Sales tax applicable in N.Y.
** Canadian residents will be charged applicable provincial taxes and GST.
All orders subject to approval. Offer limited to one per household.
® are registered trademarks of Harlequin Enterprises Limited.

PRES99   ©1998 Harlequin Enterprises Limited

 **HARLEQUIN®**
Makes any time special™

WIN A DREAM

In celebration of Harlequin®'s golden anniversary

Enter to win a *dream!* You could win:

- A luxurious trip for two to *The Renaissance Cottonwoods Resort* in Scottsdale, Arizona, or

- A bouquet of flowers once a week for a year from **FTD**, or

- A $500 shopping spree, or

- A fabulous bath & body gift basket, including **K-tel**'s *Candlelight and Romance* 5-CD set.

Look for **WIN A DREAM** flash on specially marked Harlequin® titles by Penny Jordan, Dallas Schulze, Anne Stuart and Kristine Rolofson in October 1999*.

FTD

RENAISSANCE.
COTTONWOODS RESORT
SCOTTSDALE, ARIZONA

K·TEL

"This book is DYNAMITE!"
—Kristine Rolofson

"A riveting page turner…"
—Joan Elliott Pickart

"Enough twists and turns to keep everyone
guessing… What a ride!"
—Jule McBride

See what all your favorite authors
are talking about.

Coming October 1999 to a retail store near you.

Coming Next Month

HARLEQUIN PRESENTS®

THE BEST HAS JUST GOTTEN BETTER!

#2061 THE MISTRESS ASSIGNMENT Penny Jordan
(Sweet Revenge/Seduction)
Kelly has agreed to act the seductress in order to teach a
lesson to the man who betrayed her best friend. It's a scheme
fraught with danger—especially when gorgeous stranger
Brough Frobisher gets caught in the cross fire....

#2062 THE REVENGE AFFAIR Susan Napier
(Presents Passion)
Joshua Wade was convinced that Regan was plotting to disrupt
their wedding. Regan had to admit there was unfinished
business between them—a reckless one-night stand.... She had
good reason for getting close to Joshua, though, but she could
never reveal her secret plans....

#2063 SLADE BARON'S BRIDE Sandra Marton
(The Barons)
When Lara Stevens and Slade Baron were both facing an
overnight delay in an airport, Slade suggested they spend the
time together. Who would she hurt if Lara accepted his
invitation? He wanted her, and she wanted . . . his child!

#2064 THE BOSS'S BABY Miranda Lee
(Expecting!)
When Olivia's fiancé ditched her, her world had been blown
apart and with it, her natural caution. She'd gone to the office
party and seduced her handsome boss! But now Olivia has a
secret she dare not tell him!

#2065 THE SECRET DAUGHTER Catherine Spencer
Soon after Joe Donnelly's sizzling night with Imogen Palmer,
she'd fled. Now ten years on, Joe was about to uncover an
astonishing story—one that would culminate in a heartrending
reunion with the daughter he never knew he had.

#2066 THE SOCIETY GROOM Mary Lyons
(Society Weddings)
When Olivia meets her former lover, rich socialite Dominic
FitzCharles, at a society wedding, he has a surprise for her: he
announces their betrothal to the press, in front of London's
elite. Just how is Olivia supposed to say no?